"But He may not want me to find the coins." She leaned back and crossed her arms.

"Then, if that's true, that's the path you should choose because God wants what's best for you." He placed his arm on the back of the seat behind her, his face just inches from hers. "And so do I." Mahogany eyes bored into hers so deeply she felt them prick her heart.

While still a breath apart, he said, "Good night, Meranda. Know that I pray for you every day and will say a special prayer tonight." Then he was gone. Her lips tingled as if he had kissed her, and she felt a little miffed that he hadn't.

That night, the sheets tangled her legs as she tossed in bed, wrestling with whether she should give up and hand her dream—Pop's dream—over to God or fate or whatever it was called. No. As long as she was in control, she knew she'd find them eventually.

D0827415

KATHLEEN E. KOVACH and her husband, Jim, raised two sons while living the nomadic lifestyle for over twenty years in the Air Force. She's a grandmother, though much too young for that. Now firmly planted in Colorado, she's a member of American Christian Fiction Writers and leads a local writers group. Kathleen hopes her readers will giggle through her books while learning the spiritual truths God has placed there. Visit her Web site at www.kathleenekovach.com.

Books by Kathleen E. Kovach

HEARTSONG PRESENTS
HP717—Merely Players
HP870—God Gave the Song

Don't miss out on any of our super romances. Write to us at the following address for information on our newest releases and club information.

Heartsong Presents Readers' Service
PO Box 721
Uhrichsville, OH 44683

Or visit www.heartsongpresents.com

Crossroads Bay

Kathleen E. Kovach

Heartsong Presents

I dedicate this book to my treasure, Jim.

I would also like to thank my sister, mother, and brother-in-law for willingly becoming tour guides and sharing their love of Oregon with me. Special acknowledgments go to my critique partners and to my readers, Angie Scohy and Gloria Clover. Also to those who helped me research that of which this landlubber knew nothing: Genevra Bonati, who knows boats, and Bonnie Doran and Peter Lyddon, who know diving.

A note from the Author:
I love to hear from my readers! You may correspond with me by writing:

Kathleen E. Kovach
Author Relations
PO Box 721
Uhrichsville, OH 44683

ISBN 978-1-60260-773-6

CROSSROADS BAY

Copyright © 2010 by Kathleen E. Kovach. All rights reserved. Except for use in any review, the reproduction or utilization of this work in whole or in part in any form by any electronic, mechanical, or other means, now known or hereafter invented, is forbidden without the permission of Heartsong Presents, an imprint of Barbour Publishing, Inc., PO Box 721, Uhrichsville, Ohio 44683.

Scripture taken from the HOLY BIBLE, NEW INTERNATIONAL VERSION®. NIV®. Copyright © 1973, 1978, 1984 by International Bible Society. Used by permission of Zondervan. All rights reserved.

Scripture quotations are taken from the King James Version of the Bible.

All of the characters and events in this book are fictitious. Any resemblance to actual persons, living or dead, or to actual events is purely coincidental.

Our mission is to publish and distribute inspirational products offering exceptional value and biblical encouragement to the masses.

PRINTED IN THE U.S.A.

one

Meranda Drake stood on her boat docked at the Crossroads Bay Marina and saluted the lighthouse on the hill as she'd done every morning since the accident.

"Big day, Pop." She addressed the tall structure while hugging her arms. "I'm taking a whale-watching tour out on the boat this morning. It's a twenty-fifth wedding anniversary party. Remember how you loved those?"

Her dad, the romantic who had lived for adventure.

And that adventure had taken his life a year ago tomorrow. On her birthday. Thirty-one candles had melted down to pitiful, multicolored pools of wax. She closed her eyes and swallowed the fatherless void that lodged in her throat, not ready to think about the events that led to that day. Instead, through sheer will, happier times began to surface, slowly, like bubbles from a sea turtle. She could almost hear him singing to her—"My Bonnie lies over the ocean. . ."—and hear him call her *Bonnie-girl*. She may have been a tomboy, but she was a daddy's girl. "Thank you for teaching me the trade, for sharing everything you knew about sailing." Yes, seawater had run through Pop's veins, and now Meranda felt the brine flowing through hers as well.

She glanced at her watch. The catering crew was due in a few minutes. She needed to perform her last-minute checks before taking the boat out. Her deckhand would arrive shortly. Ethan, the young college kid she'd hired after Pop died, knew boats like most people knew their phone numbers. He also interacted well with the passengers, which meant Meranda didn't have to.

She ducked her head to go below, but *arrgh. . .arrgh. . .*

sounded from her duffel bag. She pulled out her cell phone and answered it, silencing the pirate ringtone. "Drake here."

"Must you answer like a guy?"

"Hi, sis." As she talked, she wandered to the side of the boat and leaned on the rail. "Good thing you caught me before I set sail. What's up?"

"First of all, your name is Meranda, not *Drake*." Rose lowered her voice like a man.

"Did you call to harass me?"

"No. I'm sorry. I just wanted to be sure you're coming this evening."

Blast! She forgot. "Of course! I have it all worked out." *Let's see. The tour ends at four o'clock, quick shower. . .*

"I know this isn't your thing, but you have to be here. Mom is already driving me nuts."

"You shouldn't let her do that, Rose. It's your wedding. Do what you want."

"I wish I could just take to the sea like you when she rattles my nerves." She paused. "Please don't bail on me."

"I was going to research the coins more tonight. Check out the interlibrary loan since I've exhausted ours."

"The coins? Still? When are you going to give up on that myth?"

"It's not a myth. Pop believed in them."

The silence on the other end screamed, *Pop was a fool.*

Instead, Rose mercifully dropped the subject and got back to her present angst. "You know Mom. It's not my wedding anymore. It's turning into an event where I don't even have to show up. I need you tonight for backup."

"Is Steven's mother going to be there, too?"

Meranda heard a long drawn-out breath with a slight sob on the end. "Yes."

"Then I can't in good conscience let the sharks have you. I'll be your buffer."

"Thank you!"

"I'll come, make some lame suggestions. Everyone will roll their eyes and look at me like they've never seen a tomboy before."

"You're the brother I never had, Mer. And I'm proud to call you sis."

They said good-bye after more profuse thanks from Rose. Meranda glanced back at the lighthouse. "That was Rose, Pop." The lighthouse stood straight, twinkling its one eye. "Your middle child is getting married. I don't know if he's right for her. Sure wish you were here to advise her. All Mom sees is good money. You know how she is."

The light blinked once more, then stopped, the sensor sleeping now that the sun had pursued the last of night's shadow toward the western horizon.

"She's talkin' to herself again." The voice came from a neighboring boat.

Meranda frowned. *And you're as boneheaded as a backward blowfish.* Perhaps she should keep her phone to her ear while talking to the lighthouse. On a day as still as today, her voice drifted too easily to the other boats docked nearby.

"Loony as her old man." An answering voice from a different boat.

Meranda looked at the lighthouse and whispered, "We'll show 'em, Pop. We'll prove you weren't crazy."

"Hello on the boat," a female voice lilted from the dock. "We're the caterers. Permission to come aboard?"

Meranda raised her eyebrow. Good etiquette. She liked that. She waved at the young woman in black pants and white shirt who boarded with gazelle-like movements. "I'm Jessie Kingston, Paul Godfrey's assistant." She motioned toward the dock. A dark-haired man dressed the same as Jessie tipped his head toward her, then disappeared inside a white van with TAPAS MEDITERRANEAN DELIGHTS in black script painted on the side. "Where would you like us to set up?"

Meranda showed her the dining cabin, then led her to the galley. "Have you ever catered on a boat before?"

"No, but my dad owns one. So I'm quite comfortable."

"Kingston. Are you related to Phil Kingston?"

Jessie smiled. "My dad."

"No wonder you look familiar. Your dad was with mine when. . ." Looking into Jessie's hazel eyes, very much like her father's, caused a lump to form in Meranda's throat.

"Yes. Dad was on that last dive with your father. He tried to save him."

After an awkward silence, Meranda asked, "So, the last time I saw you was about ten years ago? That first meeting when my father started gathering his salvage crew. Your hair was long then. No wonder I didn't recognize you right away."

They wandered to the galley while they talked. "That sounds about right. I was sixteen. After I graduated from high school I went out of state to college, then to Paris to study the culinary arts."

"Wow, I'm impressed."

"When I came back, Paul Godfrey was looking for a sous chef, and I got the job. Then when our client said they wanted us to cater on a boat, I thought of you. I had heard you'd continued your father's business."

"Thank you. I'll try to reciprocate if I hear of anyone needing a caterer."

Meranda showed Jessie around the galley, then excused herself. "I need to test the generator before we sail. Do you need help here first?"

Jessie glanced around. "No, I think we've got it. It will be a simple setup."

"Okay, holler if you need me."

She left Jessie, trying to imagine the bubbly teen she'd met. She now sported a brown boy cut that looked easy to manage in a stiff wind. Meranda's fingers tugged the scarf on her own head—the only thing keeping her unruly curls from whipping her face. But Pop loved her long red hair, said she looked like a wild and free lady pirate. Soon the anniversary party arrived, and from topside Meranda watched Ethan help them board. The couple looked to be in their late forties, his hair dusted lightly with gray, hers a short brown flip. Another man carrying a Bible followed, probably the minister to help them renew their vows. Behind them were a dozen men, women, and a couple of older teenaged girls. Daughters, perhaps?

Just before they weighed anchor, the caterer boarded, having let his assistant do most of the setup inside.

Meranda stood on the bridge and took the helm, her heart rushing forward in the open air, creating its own wake. She never felt more alive than when the water slapped the boat as she cut her way through it.

The morning fog burned away to reveal gentle waters. Most spring days, the Oregon coast lay blanketed in haze, the occasional squall the only disturbance.

They reached the spot where she'd seen a pod of whales the day before. She cut the engines and called down to Ethan to inform the passengers to keep their eyes open.

Below were her private quarters where a tiny room held a table with two chairs on either side. A window above the table provided light and a chance for her to sit, have a cup of coffee, and keep watch of the changing Oregon weather.

Her laptop called to her, but she knew she couldn't log on to research the coins this far out at sea. Her phone card only reached about a mile off the coast.

She shuffled through the papers she'd printed previously, but held little hope. The elusive coins foiled her at every turn.

Besides the gentle lapping ocean against the wooden hull, she heard the drone of the minister near the bow. Let the renewing of the vows commence. And she heard gagging aft. She wrinkled her nose and went to the stern to investigate.

❧

"Make it stop. . . . Dear God. . .make it stop." Paul Godfrey draped his body over the hull praying someone would end his misery and push him into the Pacific Ocean.

No career was worth this. No amount of money would ever prompt him to accept a catering job on a boat again. No grandmother, despite the rock-hard determination in her diminutive body, could ever again make him do something he knew he'd regret.

His stomach gurgled again, and he clamped his lips together. Who was he kidding? He had about as much chance of resisting his grandmother's will as he did controlling the upheaval in his abdomen.

His *abuelita* hadn't really retired from the restaurant business. She'd just found a new lackey.

"You okay there, Mr. Godfrey?"

A gentle hand pressed his back. He discreetly wiped his mouth with his handkerchief and turned to look into the most beautiful eyes he'd ever seen. Stormy gray, the color of the churning sea. He glanced over the side at the gentle rhythmic swell of the water that mocked him. Well, it *should* have been churning by the way he felt.

"Um, yeah." He ordered his body to straighten and slipped the handkerchief into his pocket, trying to look as if his guts weren't floating away on the tide. "Just enjoying the view." Or rather, concentrating on the Crossroads Bay lighthouse on shore to the east. It was the only solid thing in his line of vision.

She narrowed those striking eyes and handed him a paper cup of water. "Landlubber, eh?"

"Severely."

"Take anything?"

"Seasick medicine makes me comatose." The last time he ventured on the water was to make sure his girlfriend didn't end up in the arms of another man. A group was going on a jetboat excursion on the Rogue River. Despite his sacrifice, he ended up losing her anyway. But he later felt at peace. God had other plans for his life.

"Come with me." The captain walked away, a vision in tall black boots, blue form-fitting trousers, and a billowy blouse. Her russet hair escaped the black scarf tied around her head. Yes. God had other plans. And right now being available seemed like a good idea.

Laughter floated on the air from the anniversary party at the front of the boat. All seemed to enjoy his food and were unaffected by the fact that every plank beneath their feet was rocking to the waves. Granted, even the slightest movement on the water turned Paul into a nauseated mess. He drew in a deep breath, but when the fish-laced salt air invaded his nasal passages, he felt the familiar reflex in his jaw glands signaling another episode. He swallowed convulsively to keep it at bay and concentrated on the captain's striking figure as she walked away. Mercifully, the nausea ebbed back to where it had originated. New plan. Keep eyes on the tall, beautiful skipper.

She turned and quirked her brow. "Coming? Or would you rather your customers see you upchucking? I don't nurse every seasick landlubber who dares to come aboard my ship."

He snapped to attention, resisting the urge to salute, and willed his feet to follow her. She led him below deck, where he feared his condition would worsen.

"Sit." She motioned to a chair at the small table strewn with maps and other papers. He obeyed, and she sat across from him. "Hold your hands out, wrists up."

"Are you going to scuttle me?"

"You scuttle a ship, not a wrist." As her lashes lifted, he

noticed a faint green hue in her irises that had not been there before. Intriguing. Perhaps the seaweed green walls surrounding them had something to do with it.

She took both of her thumbs and placed them on his veins where they formed a *V*. As she applied gentle pressure, he felt the nausea recede.

"Thanks. I'm feeling better. An old sea captain's remedy?"

"No, I think they used ale for most every complaint."

"Ah. The drunker the sailor, the less he feels."

She offered a half smile and those gray green eyes actually twinkled. "Something like that."

The papers under his arms drew his attention. They looked like printouts from the Internet. Some with pictures of old coins, others with maps, still others with drawings of old ships with sails.

She must have noticed him looking at them because she let his wrists go and started straightening them up. "That should help you for a moment."

"Only a moment?"

Excusing herself, she stood and walked out, then returned a few seconds later with a can of lemon-lime soda. "This will help, too. It's not ale, though. Sorry."

"That's okay. I'm not a drinker." He popped open the tab and sipped, allowing the sweet bubbles to soothe his stomach. "Thanks." He waited for her to sit across from him at the table, then made eye contact again. "I'm Paul, by the way."

"Meranda Drake." She grinned and held out her hand.

Her grip felt as solid as the woman herself, contrasting the gentle pressure she'd just applied to his wrists. In his line of work he often met frilly females wanting to either gain an advantage over their rich friends or prove their social status. Not that he minded. They were his bread and butter. This woman, however, clearly danced to her own tune. And he suspected that tune came from a hornpipe.

Excited voices above drew his attention. The room suddenly dipped to the right. He gripped the chair. "What's happening?"

Her gaze darted up the short steps leading to the deck. "They must have seen a whale spout and all rushed starboard to look at it. You want to join them?"

He wrapped one foot around the leg of the chair. "No thank you. I've seen spouts from shore. I prefer it that way."

She frowned. "Why did you take this job then?"

The question challenged his professional integrity. "My catering business comes before my personal needs." *Plus Abuelita made me.*

A knock sounded from the stairs, and Jessie ducked her head into the opening. "Excuse me," she said as her eyes adjusted to the dimmer light. "Is Paul in here? Oh, there you are." She grimaced. "You don't look so good."

"I'm fine, Jessie. What do you need?"

"The couple wants you to make an appearance so they can thank you personally for the food."

Paul groaned.

"Uh, do you want me to say you can't make it right now?" Jessie's face fell.

"I'm coming. Just give me a moment."

Jessie looked from Paul to Meranda, lingering on the captain for just an instant. "Okay." She disappeared back through the rectangular opening.

He turned back to Meranda. "Just out of cooking school."

She nodded, but he could tell she wasn't interested.

"I think I can do this." He pushed himself from the chair.

She cocked an eyebrow. "Are you sure?"

His knees wobbled but held his weight. "We'll soon see." He gingerly crept up the stairs into the bright sunlight. Before allowing his gaze to drift toward the bobbing horizon, he closed his eyes and felt the sun's rays on his face. He thanked God for the beautiful day. It could have been a wet, miserable voyage. But God smiled down and delivered. Now, if He could just freeze the ocean so the boat would stop rocking. . .

26

Meranda shook her head. Seasick passengers were nothing new, but she'd never invited one to her cabin before. What was wrong with her? Was she getting soft?

She turned her attention to the papers on the table. *Now, where are you?* She rifled through the printouts as she tried to unravel clues. Her fingers lit on a printed sheet of the coins. This clue was her first in believing they were real. The round silver pendant on a chain around her neck held the same image as one side of the coins: two pillars that looked like rooks on a chessboard with ocean waves between them, as if someone had captured a photo on a stormy day from shore. But unfortunately that had also been the last clue she had unearthed. Looking for sixteenth-century gold coins in several countries and oceans and time periods was worse than looking for buried treasure. No *X* marked the spot.

A retching sound interrupted her thoughts. *Not again.*

She raced up the steps to see Paul hanging over the side of the boat. He turned his head when he noticed her. "They said they liked the salmon puffs."

two

Once they docked and the guests departed, Meranda left Ethan to swab down the deck and lock up. She helped the caterers load the van since Paul had to stop every few minutes and moan. The poor guy had nothing left in his stomach.

Before they drove away, Meranda grasped the edge of the rolled-down van window. "You're sure you're okay?" Paul's gray face reminded her of a winter sky.

"I'm fine. Jessie will get me home."

She waved to them as they left the parking lot and stepped into her pickup. In a few minutes, her modest bungalow came into view. It had been her father's before he married Mom. Afterward he'd use it as a retreat during the rough stages of their marriage. Meranda moved into it a few years ago—also to get away from Mom.

It sat on a hillside with a view of the ocean off the deck. And best of all, three-quarters of the tall, white stucco lighthouse could be seen to the south, reaching over the trees as if it were craning its neck to look for Meranda.

After her shower she slipped into her land clothes: khaki slacks, pale blue striped, tailored shirt over a blue tank top, and brown oxfords. She towel-dried her hair on the deck, waiting for the sensor in the lighthouse to awaken and signal a safe harbor. As soon as it winked at her, she waved, then left for Mom's house.

She arrived at the family mansion, actually an upper middle class Victorian. Nothing but the best for her mother. It had been a fun place for her and her sisters to grow up, with plenty of room for hide-and-seek and wooden floors to slide on in their socks. But now as she looked at the facade, she sensed sadness. The bickering under its roof had long silenced, but it still echoed within its walls.

Her pickup looked out of place among the BMWs and other status cars in the driveway. It seemed everyone else had arrived, which meant Rose would have her head.

Inside she hung up her jacket and walked past the parlor where baby sis, twenty-four-year-old Julianne, sat surrounded by the other bridesmaids, their frilly hairdos flopping in excitement. Julianne looked up with her sparkling eyes. "Hi, Mer! We're looking through brides magazines searching for the perfect design for our dresses. I hope you don't mind looking like a girl for a day."

Please, harpoon me now.

In the dining room, noisy seagulls fought for attention over one lone pigeon, Rose. She broke away from Mom, her mother-in-law-to-be, and Aunt Vera and swooped onto Meranda, grabbing her in a hug. "I'm so glad you're here. My anchor in the storm."

"Well, that's excessive, isn't it?" Meranda patted her sister's back, then squirmed out of the clinging arms.

Rose looked behind her at the three older women, screeching at each other. Meanwhile, the puffins were peeping away in the parlor.

Or maybe not so excessive. It appeared Meranda had her work cut out for her.

Mom looked up from the table and dragged her into the fray without even a hello. "We need to discuss colors. It will all make sense once we get the colors down." She wielded a quilt's worth of swatches.

"I need a decision on the church," Mrs. St. James, Rose's soon-to-be mother-in-law, interrupted. "If we choose ours, there are certain colors that simply will not go."

"Then the same can be said about the flowers," Aunt Vera

wailed. Uncle Rex owned a florist shop, which automatically made his wife an expert.

Meranda took her captain's stance in the entry between the dining room and the parlor. With feet apart, back straight, and two fingers in her mouth, she blew a shrill whistle, gaining everyone's wide-eyed, open-mouthed attention.

With her hands on her hips, she spoke to Rose hovering behind her. "What do you want to attack first?"

"Colors." Rose's voice held a resigned tone, as if giving her mother first shot irked her. "In my mind it makes more sense to pick them first."

"Fine. Jules!" Julianne whipped her curls as she turned to look at her from the parlor. "Would you four mind keeping it down so we can think in here? Aunt Vera, we'll get to you soon. Mrs. St. James. . ." Meranda paused to see if the groom's mother would correct her, giving permission to use her first name. She didn't. "Mrs. St. James, please help yourself to some coffee, and we'll discuss the church in a little while."

The fiftyish woman, whose pronounced nose and floppy skin on her throat gave her a pelican look, huffed into the kitchen.

"Okay, enough of this nonsense." Mom grabbed Meranda's arm and hauled her to a chair. "Here's our problem." Mom reached for a pink swatch. "This is the primary color you want to go with, correct?"

Rose nodded.

"It's pink!" Meranda's throat constricted. She would not wear a pink dress. Not even for family.

"It's rose." Her sister pushed out her lower lip. Seriously? At her age? "And it's my favorite color. I want that for my maid of honor."

Mom held the pink swatch under Meranda's chin and fluffed her hair so it lay on top. "See? She looks hideous."

"Thanks, Mom."

"You know what I mean. It's not you—it's the color. There is so much red in your hair." She stroked Meranda's head and slid a lock through her fingers. "So much like your father's." Sadness crept into her eyes. It must have been tough for her mother to plan her daughter's wedding a year after losing her ex-husband, no matter how much they had fought. But she apparently stuffed that emotion away as she barked at Rose. "Do you see what I mean?"

"Yes." Rose raised her hands in frustration. "Maybe we can compromise. What if we do some kind of cape or collar in green?" She slid a green swatch over the pink one still under Meranda's chin.

Meranda looked down. "I'll look like a strawberry."

This set Rose into a fit of hysterical laughter. Mom soon joined her, and before long the whole wedding party engaged in a giggling mass of released pressure.

"Let's table this." Rose wiped her eyes. "Maybe if we look at the design we'll get a better idea of how to dress our strawberry."

Meranda groaned. It was going to be a long night.

❧

Finally alone, Paul sank onto his leather sofa with a cup of ginger tea to settle his stomach. Jessie had dropped him off, offering to take the equipment back to the restaurant. Grateful, he let her go before requesting she not tell his grandmother about his seasickness. Abuelita would no doubt call and make it all about the restaurant. Then again, perhaps she would take him seriously the next time he declined a job on a boat.

Every time he thought of the day, his stomach cramped. But when he thought of Meranda Drake, and those amazing eyes, he felt tons better. So he concentrated on the fascinating woman clad in an outfit suspiciously similar to what the pirates wore in that movie he saw last summer.

He wished he weren't so shy. Something about the woman appealed to him in a frightening way. Far from his last love interest, Ruthanne, who had married his stepcousin, Meranda didn't seem the least bit interested in being feminine. But she exuded it in a very Maureen O'Hara sort of way. He chuckled. Like that movie he saw the other night, *Sinbad the Sailor*. He stroked an imaginary beard. Could he ever be as dashing as Douglas Fairbanks Jr.?

He sipped the tea and burned his tongue as his home phone rang. Setting the cup aside, he answered. "Hello."

"Pablo."

"*Hola*, Abuelita."

"Jessie tells me you are ill. The crab was not bad, was it? We do not need a lawsuit." Yep. His little Spanish grandma made it all about the restaurant.

"I'm fine, just a little seasick. I'll eat a few crackers before I go to bed, and I'll be good as new tomorrow."

"I will be at the restaurant early in case you don't make it. You are catering a brunch, *sí*?"

"Yes, but you don't have to do that. I'll be there."

"You are fixing my *magdalena* recipe, *sí*?"

"Yes, Abuelita. I will do the cakes justice."

"I will come and help."

Paul wished he could tell her to retire already. That had been the bargain. That's why he had made the decision to move back home. His cousin, Albert, had agreed to comanage the restaurant while Paul set up his catering business out of the kitchen. Both men were frustrated with their grandmother. But how could they kick her out of the restaurant she and Grandpa had built from scratch?

They hung up, Paul not convincing her that he could handle the brunch by himself. He lifted the now-cooled ginger tea and sipped it. The way his stomach felt, he wondered if he'd picked up a flu bug.

He reached for his Bible. The thought of turning on the television occurred to him, but he hoped he could glean something from scripture on how to handle an old woman.

His cell phone rang, halting his hand. He dragged himself from the chair and trudged to the small round table where he always deposited his keys and phone when he walked into the house.

"Hello, Paul Godfrey speaking."

"Is this Paul the caterer?"

He knew that voice. "Yes."

"Hi. This is Meranda Drake. You were on my boat today?"

"Yes, Miss Drake. An experience I'll not soon forget." He rubbed his stomach and lounged back down on the couch.

She offered a hearty laugh, and strangely it didn't offend him in the least. "I hope you're feeling better."

"Much." *Now.*

"I'm helping my sister plan her wedding, and talk turned to the caterer. Our mother's usual one got deported last month. France. Apparently it was quite upsetting."

"I can imagine. Two questions though. Will it be on a boat?"

Again, that laugh—like a burst of sunshine. "No, I promise."

"Then I'll be happy to talk with her about it. Second question: when is it?"

"In a year, May twenty-eighth."

He raised his gaze to the ceiling as if his planning calendar was tacked up there. "I'm sure I have that date free. We could meet Monday morning at my grandmoth—my family's restaurant, Tapas." If he were to declare emancipation, he needed to start weaning Abuelita away, starting with his thoughts. "Around nine? We're not open for breakfast, so I take my catering clients in the morning. I hope *you'll* be there." Did that bold statement just come from him? "I mean. . .that is. . ."

"I can't come." Two different women argued in the background. Meranda told them both to settle it themselves.

Then she came back on. "I have a tour, but my sister can make it. . .and apparently so will my mother."

After they said good-bye, Paul contemplated what a family of Merandas would look like.

❧

"May I go home now?" Meranda had done her social duty and hooked her mother up with a respected caterer. At least she assumed so since he had the name of his business painted on his van.

"I still wish we could use Philippe. He was the best caterer I knew." What her mother really meant was that he was the most popular among her friends and therefore would stamp her social passport.

By the end of the planning party, Rose managed to keep her favorite color with a contrasting shade of pink that everyone agreed didn't look as "hideous" on Meranda. Except Meranda. The church was settled on, the flowers agreed upon, and the bridesmaids couldn't be happier with the design of their dresses.

Before Meranda left, she found Julianne on her knees searching through the cherrywood buffet, her strawberry curls jittering as she rooted inside.

"What are you looking for?" Meranda asked.

"The silver candlesticks. Doesn't Mom keep them in here?"

Their mother lingered over coffee in the parlor with Mrs. St. James.

"Mom!" Julianne called from the dining room.

"Julianne, don't bellow," Mom roared, breaking her own rule. "Come here to talk to me."

Julianne bounced into the parlor. Meranda stood near the entry and watched their exchange.

"Where are the silver candlesticks?"

"Why do you want them?"

"They probably need to be polished. Won't we use them

for the shower or something?"

"I sold them. They weren't really my style." Mom waved her hand, dismissing the subject.

Irritation boiled in Meranda's stomach. The candlesticks were Nana Drake's. Mom should have passed them down. Meranda didn't care for them, but by Julianne's pout, they seemed important to her.

A thought hit Meranda, though. Did Mom need funds for the wedding? Didn't she receive a small inheritance from her father? Or had she squandered it while keeping up with her society friends? The way she spent money often alarmed Meranda. She pulled Julianne and Rose aside. They stood in the kitchen and kept their voices low.

"Julianne," Meranda started the brief parley. "Have you noticed anything else missing from the house?"

"Yes." The corners of her mouth dipped. "More of Nana's antiques, like her silver tea set, her jewelry, the vanity set with the matching brush and mirror."

"And some artwork," Rose contributed, "that had belonged to Grandma Muldoon."

"So, she's not only getting rid of things that remind her of Pop, but her own side of the family's as well."

They both nodded.

"Girls." Meranda placed her hands on both their shoulders. "Mom's in trouble."

"Should we confront her now?" The trepidation in Rose's eyes clearly suggested it wouldn't be she doing the confronting.

Meranda peeked out the kitchen door. Mrs. St. James continued to drone in the parlor. No telling when she would go home.

"Let's just monitor the situation for now, okay?" She doubted confronting Mom would do any good anyway.

She said good-bye to Mom and Mrs. St. James. As she headed for the door, Rose followed her.

"Thanks for coming, Mer." Rose hugged Meranda with the ferocity of a circus bear.

"I'm glad I could help. I may not be able to tell a lily from a dahlia, but I can manage a rowdy crew."

"That was the gift I needed." Rose's eyes went wide. "Gift! Meranda, tomorrow is your birthday."

A small dagger pricked her heart. She had hoped since no one mentioned it, they might have been planning to surprise her.

"I'm so sorry. We're so caught up in this wedding."

Meranda patted her sister's shoulder. "Don't worry about it."

"But Mom should have—"

"It's okay. She will also be dealing with another anniversary tomorrow. If she remembers me, fine. If not, I'm not worried about it."

"You, me, and Jules—and Mom if she feels up to it. Tomorrow for dinner. Okay?"

"Sure."

Meranda grabbed her jacket from the closet and picked up her duffel. Just as she was heading out, she noticed the mail sitting on the credenza by the door. The corner of a large manila envelope stuck out from under the bills. It was from the Crossroads Bay Maritime Museum and addressed to her father. She looked over her shoulder to see if her mother was watching, then slid it into her bag. Julianne had probably brought in the mail, and her mother hadn't seen it yet.

When she arrived home, she walked straight through the living room to Pop's metal desk that he'd bought at a navy surplus store. It sat under the back window over the balcony. The lighthouse greeted her beyond the window now that night had claimed the area.

"Look what we got, Pop." Taking a fish fillet knife, she slit the top of the envelope and spilled the contents onto the desk. The cover letter caught her eye, and she adjusted the desk lamp to read it better.

Dear Gilbert Drake,

Your request for Augustus Drake's belongings only turned up the following: news clippings and old letters sent to his sister. The Crossroads Bay Museum may have more information. I hope you find what you're searching for.

Regards,
Richard Miller
Director of Marine Artifacts

The news clippings had yellowed and seemed to document the building of the lighthouse, pictures that weren't much different from what she'd seen in the Crossroads Bay Museum. But five smaller envelopes lay among the fragile papers. They also appeared old. Her hands shook as she touched her own history. She picked up the first one and carefully pinched the letter inside to draw it out. The bold script proved difficult to read.

June 10, 1905

Dear Charlotte,

I'm sure you have heard of the loss of the Victoria Jane *and feared I may have met my end as well. I'm most happy to inform you that I am alive and healthy. Many of us survived, for which I am grateful, but I grieve the loss of the crew who valiantly braved the sea voyage from Hawaii.*

Meranda's upper lip began to sweat. This shipwreck had led to her father's demise. She read further, hoping to gain some encouragement that he hadn't died in vain.

I plan to build a lighthouse in dedication to those lost and to prevent another such accident.

I grieve not only for our brother, but also that you were not

able to go with me to officially say good-bye. All the villagers
that he ministered to loved him.

Your Faithful Brother,
Augustus

Well, so far she hadn't learned anything new. It was
common knowledge that her great-great-grandfather had
lost a ship coming back from Hawaii. It was also known that
he had an older brother and that Charlotte was their sister
living in San Francisco.

She opened the other letters, all dated later and giving
updates to Charlotte on the lighthouse. The last letter would
have to hold a clue, or nothing in this package was worth
anything to her.

July 2, 1907

Dear Charlotte,
As you know, with the untimely demise of our brother,
I became the keeper of The Inheritance.

Meranda hopped out of the chair and let out a whoop.
"Happy birthday to me!" Then she stood while she read the
rest.

I brought it back from Hawaii with me and want you to
know that it is safe, and I'm concretely sure it is where no one
will find it.

"This is it, Pop! Augustus says it's safe. That rules out the
shipwreck, right?"
The lighthouse winked.
The rest of the letter had to do with personal stuff. He'd
met a woman, they were getting married. That union no
doubt led to her grandfather's birth.

Meranda sat down to think. The lighthouse property was sold after Augustus's death. That owner had a falling out with Grandpa, who had moved out by then, and refused to let him back onto the property. No owner since would allow anyone past the gate that had been built to keep people out.

She needed to change that. Somehow.

three

Paul's cousin Al poked his head in the kitchen doorway. "Is Abuelita here yet?"

"No, and a good thing, too." Paul grabbed some fresh parsley and scissors and began snipping the spicy-smelling greenery into the soup stock. "Sleep in?"

"Yeah. Baby kept us up all night."

"Now, Alberto." Paul squeezed into his falsetto voice and seasoned it with a Spanish accent. "Your *abuelo* and I raised seven children while working this restaurant. How can you let one tiny *bebé* keep you from doing your job?"

Al's gaze drifted past Paul and a look of terror laced his face.

Paul winced and whispered, "She's standing behind me, isn't she?"

"No, bro." Al slapped his shoulder and broke into an I-gotcha grin. "I'm just messing with you."

Paul grabbed his chest. "Don't do that!"

"Hey,"—Al threw on his apron and chef's hat—"thanks for starting the base foods for me."

"Again."

"Again."

"Not a problem." Paul looked at his watch. "I have an appointment coming in about five minutes. After that I can help with lunch."

"Hey, isn't today your day off?"

Paul held his palms out and shrugged. "I've got nowhere to go. I'll help out here."

"Man, we've got to get you a girlfriend." Al waved him off with a disgusted frown.

Paul left the kitchen buoyed with thoughts of Meranda.

Mrs. Drake and Meranda's sister arrived on time. After introductions he led them to a table in the empty dining room.

"Let's sit near the window. It's dark in here."

Rose gazed around. "Yes, but I love the dark wood and the rich red walls. It all looks so. . .Spanish."

Paul chuckled. "Well, that's the look we're going for."

The two women sat in the wooden ladder-back chairs. Rose sniffed the air. "Smells like you're already cooking."

"We open at eleven for lunch. We only use homemade ingredients here, so what you smell is the soup stock."

He looked from mother to daughter trying to pick out a family resemblance to Meranda. Only a hint of the tall beauty showed on her mother's face—same nose and lips. Her sister had the same arched brows, and her eyes showed more green, but they didn't flash like Meranda's.

Before he stared too long, he opened his three-ring binder with menu choices. He focused on the bride, as he always tried to do. "At Tapas, we are known for the traditional Spanish appetizers that make a whole meal. Would you like to go that route, or would you rather stick with a three-course dinner?"

Rose began to answer, but her mother interrupted her. "We're very traditional in our family. Let's stick with three courses."

"Mothers often want to go with tradition, but we want this to be about the bride, right?" He made a point of addressing the bride-to-be. "Rose, is that your preference?"

Mrs. Drake slid her hand on the table in front of Rose and leaned forward. "Do you have anything French?"

"Mother! We're in a Spanish restaurant."

The older woman glanced around as if seeing her surroundings for the first time. "Yes, so we are."

"If I may. . ." Paul addressed Rose again. "I have a wide repertoire of dishes. My specialty is Spanish cuisine, but I can provide anything you'd like."

Rose glanced at her mother, her chin jutted forward. "I like the thought of several appetizers. Then the guests can mingle or sit if they wish."

"Mm." Paul tented his fingers and touched his lips. "Very European."

Mrs. Drake tilted her head slightly. "I think the Van de Horns had a similar party. But we can't do spicy. Remember your great-aunt Vera's gallbladder."

"I'd rather not think of Aunt Vera's gallbladder while I'm getting married, Mom."

The tension between these two women could be stabbed with a fork, run through a meat grinder, and still be indigestible. Paul leaned back in his chair. "Spanish food is not so much spicy as flavorful. I have plenty of nonspicy foods to choose from."

Rose's mother huffed and looked at Paul. "What do you suggest?"

"A mix of Spanish and other fare? Some with a kick, some not?"

She tipped her head. "If you will."

Paul raised his eyebrow at Rose, hoping she'd allow them to move on.

"Fine." She sighed. "Let's protect all of your friends' sensitive stomachs."

He led them through the menu, a mix of international foods. Everything Rose liked, Mrs. Drake hated, and vice versa.

"You know, Rose." Paul felt he needed to say something. "This is your wedding. You have the final say."

Mrs. Drake screwed up her face. "Cordon bleu!"

"Excuse me?"

"Cordon bleu is French. Can't you make that?" Her eyes challenged him.

"Yes, I can. Rose, what do you think?"

Rose looked from her mother to Paul. "I don't want to have anything French on the menu. That's all Mom and her friends have had at their gatherings. Let's do something fun. . . tacos!"

"Tacos?" Mrs. Drake's eyes bugged.

"I can do a taco bar." Paul caught Rose's eye and winked. She sent a small, conspiratorial smile back telegraphing her appreciation.

Mrs. Drake folded her arms. "We will not have *tacos* at my wedding."

"*My* wedding, Mother." The corners of Rose's mouth dipped.

"Of course, dear. I only meant that since I'm paying for it. . ." The excuse trailed off, but it was decidedly meant to thumbtack Rose to her place.

"You treat me like a child."

Okay. Time to check the soup. He stood. "I'll let you two talk in private for a moment."

They both ignored him.

"Of course I treat you like a child. Still living at home. Never married. Dolls on your bed." Mrs. Drake ticked each item off on her fingers. "Your new husband isn't going to put up with that, I can assure you."

Paul heard the smackdown with embarrassed interest as he retreated to the kitchen. No wonder Meranda took to the water.

Al stood at the block chopping green peppers. "What's going on in there?"

"A domestic dispute."

"Should I call someone? We don't need bloodshed. Abuelita does that enough here."

"Um. . .Al. . ." Paul pointed over Al's shoulder.

"Come on. I know she's not standing behind me." Al continued to chop.

"Alberto." Abuelita startled Al, and he nearly slit the end of his thumb.

Quickly choosing between battles, he left Al and Abuelita and joined the sparring in the dining room.

When he returned, the two women were still going at it.

He'd had enough. "I have a suggestion." Still standing, he leaned his knuckles on the table. "What if we have a contest? Invite friends here—we have a party room in the back—and vote for the dishes."

Rose recovered quickly from her verbal whipping and bounced in her chair. "I have a better idea. What if you come to our country club and put on a demonstration. I teach a cooking class there, and I'm sure they'd all love to see a professional at work."

Mrs. Drake rolled her eyes. Did she have a problem with a young socialite loving to cook? "No," she said with the guile of a fox. "Come to my house. I have a large kitchen."

Rose narrowed her eyes. "Home court advantage, Mother?"

"That sounds like a great idea." Paul quickly stepped in before another row began. He pulled out his chair and sat, then flipped through his day planner. "When?"

"This Wednesday." Again, Mrs. Drake challenged him. She probably didn't like the fact that he had been in Rose's corner throughout the meeting. Did she think he couldn't pull this off in two days?

"Wednesday is good for me." Paul penciled them in. "In fact, if you allow me to use this opportunity to let your friends know about me, I'll only charge for the food." Yep. This could be a great marketing tool. He jotted down prices for the proposal. "Make a party of it. Rose, bring your class and we'll prepare the food together. Mrs. Drake, you and your friends can relax or participate, but everyone will have a chance to vote."

Mrs. Drake stood. Conversation over. "This Wednesday.

We'll have everybody there."

No doubt. Mrs. Drake and Meranda did have something in common. They could both bark orders.

&

Wednesday evening Paul and Jessie loaded the van and drove to the upscale neighborhood where Meranda's mother lived. Was this where Meranda grew up? How did she ever become a charter boat captain?

Rose greeted them and showed them the large kitchen and dining room where they would set up.

Jessie whistled. "I like this kitchen." She wandered around the room. Pointing at the cabinets she asked, "Cherry?"

Rose nodded while caressing the marble countertop. "This is the only room in the house that I care about."

Paul decided to watch this woman. If she were any good in the culinary arts, he might have to offer her a job.

The guests began to arrive, an eclectic mix of fifty-somethings and younger, about thirty women in all. How did they pull this party off so fast?

"This could be interesting," he said to Jessie as they laid out the appetizers.

Jessie cast her gaze around the dining room at the two factions squaring off in preparation for the tasting contest. "Reminds me of *West Side Story*."

"I don't think I want to get into the middle of a rumble." Paul ducked into the kitchen and laid out his knives near the cutting board—within quick reach—in case he had to use them on the crowd.

Mrs. Drake called for everyone's attention in the dining room. Showtime. He stepped to the doorway and waited for her to introduce him. Then he continued the announcement. "Thanks for coming out to help Rose decide what food would work for the wedding. I've already prepared a sampling of approved *tapas*—that's Spanish for appetizers—so you may help yourselves while I give a cooking demonstration in the kitchen."

Jessie had set out his business cards in strategic places throughout the house, and the pile on the table had already started to dwindle. Rumble or not, he felt this night would be a success for his business.

The women began milling about, nabbing bits of food for their plates—marinated olives, grilled eggplant, and red peppers stuffed with tuna, among a few others. Almost everyone followed him into the kitchen or watched from the pass-through as he began his demonstration. He'd laid down the rule that no one was to know which food Rose or Mrs. Drake preferred, but he suspected that each woman went to her friends privately. Hopefully his food would be so good, they wouldn't know which to pick.

"Our menu tonight, ladies, is red onion and orange salad, chicken and chorizo paella, and *empanadas*."

Fifteen people in the large kitchen oohed appreciatively. Those in the dining room clapped their appreciation.

While setting up the vegetables for chopping, Paul glanced toward the other room and caught sight of a wild red ponytail somewhat contained in a skull and crossbones barrette. A song entered his heart. *Meranda, I just met a girl named Meranda.* "Rose, aren't your sisters going to join us? Or are you the only cook in the family?"

Rose had donned a pink pastel apron and was pouring rice into a cooker. "Julianne has decided she's going to marry rich and therefore won't have need of cooking knowledge."

"And Meranda?"

The lady in question entered the kitchen holding an olive-oil-soaked piece of rye bread.

Rose laughed. "Look at her."

Meranda frowned back.

I am.

He couldn't pull his gaze from her as she set the bread on the counter and rummaged through the cabinet until she found. . .oh horrors! Peanut butter. Surely she wasn't going to ruin his bread and alioli with. . . Oh yes, she did. Paul winced.

Rose shook her head. "Mer thinks the only cooking utensils she needs are an aluminum camping kit and a pocketknife."

Meranda speared her with a glare. "You don't think I can cook?"

"Not like this." Rose cracked an egg and separated the white from the yolk, all with one hand.

Impressive. Yes, Paul would have to take notes on this one.

Meranda joined them at the freestanding counter and set her partially eaten bread down. Paul thought of slipping a plate under it but didn't want to embarrass her. She grabbed an egg and slammed it against the bowl. It *splurched* all over her hand from the violent gash.

"See?" Rose snickered.

"I can crack an egg." Meranda grabbed another one. "You just had my adrenaline pumping." She tapped the egg on its side and transferred the yolk to a bowl with only a minute slimy drip.

Paul handed her a small whisk. "Since you're here, would you mind beating that?" With Rose's egg, he showed her how to do it.

She began slow and easy, but then truly proceeded to beat the poor thing.

"No." Rose stepped in. "Not like a jackhammer."

"Allow me." Paul parted the other chefs in the kitchen and stood next to Meranda. He placed his hand on her back and took her wrist. "Like this." Together they created egg art as the yellow yolk frothed in the bowl.

If he hadn't been standing so close to her, he would have missed the clean scent of her hair. He half-expected her to smell salty.

She turned her head and met his gaze, then pulled away abruptly. "I think I have it now."

"Of course." Paul attempted to recover from her nearness, but knew he failed miserably. Surely he'd turned red as the peppers marinating in the dining room. "Uh. . .now let's brush this egg onto our empanada dough for a finished shine."

Mrs. Drake stood at the doorway. "Meranda! Are you actually. . .?"

"Cooking," Meranda finished. "Yes, Mother, I'm cooking." She grabbed an onion and a very inappropriate cleaver and proceeded to rear it back as if she were a one-armed lumberjack.

"Use this." Paul caught her arm before she lost a finger, removed the weapon, and replaced it with his ten-inch. . .no. . . eight-inch chef's knife. Meranda Drake did not need a long knife in her hand. "It has a weighted blade so it does most of the work for you."

Mrs. Drake passed Meranda on her way to a drawer where she rummaged through and pulled out a business card. "Ah. Here it is. The man who does my hair. Mrs. St. James is asking." She paused at the doorway and glanced at Meranda. "Be careful, dear. Remember the Easter fiasco." The others in the kitchen tittered along with Meranda's condescending mother. "Fruit salad. She forgot to drain off the juice. We ended up with fruit soup."

Meranda seemed to take the jibing in quiet stride, but it ticked Paul off. "She's actually doing quite well. Tell me, Mrs. Drake. Have you ever captained a ship?"

Mrs. Drake puckered like a prune. "Certainly not."

"Well, I'm sure if you ever tried, it would be as equally difficult a task. However, since you and Meranda share the same genes, I'm sure you could pick it up very easily."

Mrs. Drake started to say something, hesitated, then said,

"Thank you." Then she wandered out of the kitchen.

"That was amazing." Meranda's eyes glowed with what he hoped was admiration. "You put her in her place and complimented her at the same time. How did you do that?"

"Years of working with the public." And with women like Mrs. Drake.

A silent exchange passed between Meranda and Rose. Then the two smiled as if from the same joke.

four

Meranda squelched the urge to pump the air and shout "Yes!" after her mother walked out of the kitchen in a confused stupor. Who was this guy, anyway?

For the next half hour, she chopped, mixed, and sautéed next to Paul. Even though Rose's students were there to learn, he used Meranda often to demonstrate. Finally everything was ready to put on the table. She couldn't wait to dig into the paella. The savory rice, chicken, and sausage dish lured her out to the dining room and was the first thing she put on her plate.

She rested her back against the arched entryway that led to the parlor. As she popped a piece of sausage in her mouth, Rose sidled up to her. "I'm sorry for the ribbing I gave you earlier. You're such an easy target when it comes to domestic stuff. I really appreciate you coming over."

"It's okay. Just gives me an excuse to exchange the ice ring at your reception with one I'll add spiders to." She offered a wicked smile.

"You wouldn't dare!" She laughed, but her eyes held that tiny bit of terror that Meranda had loved eliciting since they were kids. "By the way"—Rose discreetly slipped a note into Meranda's hand— "when you vote on the food, these are the ones I really liked."

Meranda deposited it into her pants pocket. "Got it."

"Paul is something, isn't he?" Rose took a bite of the empanada.

"He can cook." Meranda also bit into an empanada, the pastry crusting just right and the shredded pork loin tasting tender and succulent.

"He's also been watching you, with interest."

Warmth infused Meranda's cheeks. "Don't be silly."

"And you've been watching back."

"Have not!"

"Have so!"

"Girls!" Mom walked by, shaking her head. "Will you never grow up?"

Meranda bumped Rose's shoulder, and Rose bumped back as they left the entryway and passed Mom on their way to the kitchen. She rolled her eyes at them as she stopped to fill her plate again.

Paul stood at the sink washing the larger pans and empty serving dishes Jessie had brought to him. There was something intriguing about a man doing dishes. Meranda felt her cheeks warm again, as they did when she spent too long topside on her boat.

Meranda slid her plate and fork onto the counter near the sink. When Paul reached for them, he dripped suds onto her hand. "Oops. Sorry." He went to wipe them off, but only transferred more bubbles.

His touch cooled and burned at the same time. She grabbed a towel. "Maybe I'd better use this."

"Um. . .yeah." His shy smile created a pleasant sensation in her stomach.

Rose leaned against the counter, a knowing smirk on her face. Meranda gave her a warning look, hoping to signal her to drop the matchmaking.

"So," Rose began. Meranda feared she'd say something to embarrass her in front of Paul. "Any luck with the coins?"

"Coins?" Mom flew into the kitchen. Was there nowhere her ears couldn't reach? "Are you still looking for those things? After what they did to your father?"

Rose's hand flew to her mouth. "I'm sorry. I thought she knew."

"Answer me." Mom's nostrils flared.

Everyone in the kitchen and dining room froze. Even the soapy drip from Paul's hand waited to hear how this all played out.

Great, let's air our dirty laundry in front of the cute guy.

Paul hastily dried his hands and excused himself from the kitchen. Although he'd never be able to go far enough to escape her mother's shrill voice.

"The coins didn't kill Pop."

"No, but his obsession did. And now you're following in his footsteps?"

"Yes, Mother." The two women locked glares. "I'm looking for the coins. They were important to Pop, and they're important to me."

"They're a myth. He died over something that doesn't exist."

But they did exist, and Meranda had proof. But she wasn't about to share that with her mother, who'd only ruin her excitement over the discovery.

"What do you care?" Meranda knew she should swallow her rushing words, but they barreled through her teeth like a northeast wind. "You had kicked him out of the house months before that. You divorced him."

Mom jerked as if she'd just been slapped. "I loved him, but. . ."

"But what? He didn't fit in with your lifestyle? You were embarrassed by him? What?"

Mom's eyes narrowed to mere slits. In a low voice, she ground through her teeth, "I won't discuss this with you now. We have guests."

The house had become very quiet. Meranda's adrenaline continued to rush through her pounding heart even as her mother strode through the now-vacant dining room and disappeared into the parlor. Remorse hit her for her harsh words. When would she learn to think before acting?

"You may all stay and vote on the food," she heard her mother say, "but I'm going to lie down. I've suddenly acquired a headache."

Rose stroked Meranda's shoulder. "I'm so sorry. I didn't know you hadn't told her."

"Well, she knows now." Meranda willed her fists to relax. "Probably a good thing. I don't have to sneak behind her back anymore." She drew in a big breath. "I'm sorry. I didn't mean to spoil your party."

"You didn't. Mom was out of line. She should have waited to confront you about the coins until everyone had left."

Meranda still felt horrible and felt the need to be near the last vestige of Pop's memory in the house—his study.

But even that was no longer his. Disgusted, she walked into the redecorated room. How long had it been since she'd been in there? Pink and green paint had erased the nautical theme. Thankfully, Meranda had already snatched his models of tall ships or they might have landed in the dumpster.

She sat in her father's favorite chair, reupholstered with a flowery eyesore. The marble-topped side table was still there but now sported a lacy doily and—what's this? A newspaper tossed casually onto the table caught her eye. Or rather, a picture of her lighthouse and an article about the owner. She picked it up and started to read.

"Judge Gordon Bernard will be giving his daughter in marriage at the Crossroads Bay lighthouse in a private ceremony." Yay. Great for them. Total strangers get onto the lighthouse property, but not the original owner's great-great-granddaughter. "Bernard recently presided over California's high-profile stalking trial of actress Trista Farentino." Meranda frowned. Leave it to the media to add a negative to a happy event.

Deciding to apologize to Paul for their fiasco, she tore the article out of the paper to explain why she and her mother had suddenly gone insane.

She left the study and searched for Paul, who stood in the dining room announcing the winners of the contest.

Blast. She had forgotten to vote. She fingered the note in her pocket, tempted to hand it to Paul. But by the glow on Rose's face, her dishes must have come out ahead anyway.

As the party broke up, she grabbed her jacket and helped Paul and Jessie load the van. "I'd like to apologize for our little drama in there."

"Believe me, that's not the first family squabble I've seen in my business."

"Maybe not, but it's the first time I've ever yelled at my mother in front of company. I don't know what got into me." Well, yes, she did. Ever since Pop's death, her animosity toward her mother had built until it finally blew at an unfortunate moment.

Changing the subject, she handed him the newspaper and pointed out the article. "This is what has me so hot under the collar. I'm frustrated that I can't get into the lighthouse my great-great-grandfather built."

"Seriously? The Crossroads Bay lighthouse?"

"Yep. And the coins you heard us arguing about? They're ancient coins, and I think he hid them in the lighthouse."

He perused the article while leaning against the van's sliding side door. "Wow. Hey, Jess, look at this."

Jessie deposited the bag of dirty towels and linens into the van and then read the article. "You should bid on this."

"You think? They might already have a caterer."

"Well, Philippe is out of the picture." Meranda reminded him of the popular caterer among her mother's friends. "They may be looking for someone at the last minute."

"And your grandmother would love it if you got the bid."

Jessie looked at Meranda and raised her eyebrows. "May I keep this?"

"Sure." The wedding announcement was nothing but a slap in the face as far as Meranda was concerned.

Paul nodded. "I'll do it. Thanks, Meranda."

"Glad I could help." She slid her fingers into the front pockets of her slacks. "I wish I could go with you and look around at the lighthouse."

"Hey," Jessie said as she thumped the page with her index finger. "If we get it, we should snoop around for Meranda."

A tingling sensation hit the back of Meranda's neck as she thought of the possibility. But then her hopes were dashed when Paul backed away from both of them, his palms raised as if pushing that idea far away. "I'll put in a bid, but I'm not going to snoop."

Jessie plopped down on the van floor and dusted the concrete driveway with her shoes. "Come on, Paul. There will be a ton of people there. No one will know if we sneak into the lighthouse."

"We?" Paul shot her an incredulous glare.

Meranda's heart beat against her chest. She had an ally in Jessie. "I'm not going to ask you to do anything you're not comfortable with. But an extra set of eyes wouldn't hurt."

"Sure." Jessie's eyes danced. "We could knock on some walls to see if there are any hidden compartments."

His lips pinched in a dubious expression. "If I get the bid, there will be no snooping, by me or Jess. We will go where we're allowed, and we're not going to knock on any walls. It's *my* reputation at stake." He stabbed his thumb toward his chest and glared at his assistant. "This judge is not known for being a nice guy."

"I know." Meranda's gaze dropped to the driveway. "Even though my ancestor built the lighthouse, Judge Bernard refuses to let our family on his property."

Meranda had often thought of scaling the fortress since the judge was rarely there. But common sense prevailed.

"Look, I'd like to help you out, but I have to protect my business." He turned to go back into the house, and Jessie followed him.

Meranda hoped she hadn't upset Paul. She'd had fun cooking with him—okay, that's something she never thought she'd say—and wanted to get to know him better.

She'd have to figure out a way to get into the lighthouse herself.

five

Meranda had piloted topside at the upper wheel on her boat while chartering a fishing tour. The afternoon had been relatively warm, with only one tiny squall to mar the trip. And now the near-cloudless sky promised a beautiful evening. With the days getting longer, she looked forward to spending more time on the water.

After she pulled into the dock, the family of seven, consisting of parents, grandparents, and three teenage sons—the oldest had developed a little crush on her—exuded their appreciation for the "highly enjoyable" tour. They insisted on taking pictures with Meranda and Ethan along with the mess of sturgeon they'd caught.

Once they left, Meranda grabbed some corn chips for her dinner and started cleaning the boat.

"Gotta run, Meranda." Ethan, who had night classes on Mondays, called to her.

"Go on." She waved him off. "I'll clean up."

He flipped on the water spigot from the dock and tossed her the hose. Then he raced to his car.

She filled a bucket with soapy water, deciding to swab the deck before rinsing off the salty sea. Not satisfied with the junk food she'd just offered her stomach, it grumbled as she thought of Paul's paella.

Her mind drifted to the tasting party last week. The guy had other good things going for him, too. She liked how he stood up to her mother. Not that she couldn't handle her mom, but it felt nice to have a man, an attractive man, do it for her. And that was the second thing he had going. Her first impression of Paul draped over her railing would not have led to her thinking about him day and night. But now she remembered his shy grin and the twinkle in his dark chocolate eyes.

As she mopped, the object of her musings sauntered toward her down the dock, hands in pockets, as if he didn't have a problem with boats. Her stomach did that funny thing again, like minnows swimming happy laps inside.

"Ahoy there." He raised his hand in greeting. "That is what you say, isn't it?"

She leaned on the mop handle and waved him on. "It'll do. Come aboard."

He stopped sauntering. "Um, no thanks. I just came to tell you something."

"Can it wait a moment? I need to finish this before the sun goes down." She dipped her mop into the bucket. "I took a family out fishing this afternoon, and the man landed a big one. It flopped around in the boat for a while. You should have seen it. That thing was this—whoops!" Her heel caught a slippery spot, and she went down hard on her hip.

Before she knew it, Paul suddenly stood above her with concern in his eyes. "Are you okay?"

"Yeah." How did he get there so fast? She allowed him to help her up. "That was just my evil plan to get you on my boat."

He looked around as if he just realized where he was. "Well, it worked." He must have noticed her rubbing her backside as she limped to a large white box on the deck and eased herself onto it. "Are you sure you're okay?"

"I think my pride is bruised. I've never fallen on this boat before."

"Maybe I distracted you."

A pleasant distraction. Yikes! She'd nearly voiced that thought. Pain throbbed into her left hip. She shifted.

"Let me bring you some ice for your, uh, pride." He disappeared below, knowing where to go after catering, and came back a moment later with a plastic bag filled with ice. "Here, sit on this a moment. I'll finish mopping."

"I can't have you do my—ow." As she started to get up, blood rushed to what she suspected would be a glorious bruise on her backside. "Watch that spot there." She pointed, and he sidestepped the slimy spot, then ran the mop over it.

"So." She readjusted the ice pack. "You have something to tell me?"

"Oh, yeah." He stopped mopping and leaned on the handle. "I got the bid."

"To the lighthouse wedding?"

"Yep."

Excitement thrummed through her. "That was quick."

He sloshed the mop into the bucket and resumed the chore. "It turns out that Judge Bernard's daughter is marrying a Lopez. Apparently, I'm the only one in town who caters authentic Spanish food."

She chewed her lip. "Wish I could be there."

"I know." He wrung out the mop. "All I can promise is that I'll keep my eyes open, but I have no idea what I'm looking for. And I'll only have access to the kitchen and patio." Paul tossed a glance at her with a curious tilt to his head. "So, tell me about the coins."

❧

Paul found himself staring at the smile that blossomed on her face and, more directly, the tiny dimple that appeared on her cheek. He jerked his attention back to the dirty deck.

"My many-times great-uncle was Sir Francis Drake."

He paused his mopping. "Really?"

She nodded, seemingly pleased by his interest. "He looted from the Spanish for the queen." Her hand flew to her mouth. "Maybe I shouldn't have mentioned that, you being Spanish and all."

She sure looked cute flustered.

"I'm also a quarter English. Last name is Godfrey, remember."

"Oh, right." She adjusted the ice pack and went on. "There's a story of a bag of coins that *somehow* didn't make it to the queen. At first they were said to bring good luck to all who possessed them."

"Do you believe that?"

"No. I'm not superstitious."

He sent up a quick prayer of thanks.

"A couple of generations later," Meranda continued, "a member of the family traveled to Spain to return them. No doubt this was the result of some unfortunate incident where the coins were blamed. The king was so moved that he returned seven of the coins and blessed them. Forever afterward they were renamed The Inheritance, and each generation of my family would hide them for the next generation to find."

"So it became a game."

"Or a way to keep them safe. I don't know."

"And they're important to you now because. . ."

"They're mine." She pressed her fist to her chest and dropped her gaze to the deck. "And because my father died searching for them." When she looked back up at him, fire flashed from her gray eyes. "The town thinks he was crazy. I need to prove to them he wasn't."

And, he surmised, judging by the way she'd been treated at the tasting party, she needed to prove she wasn't crazy as well. But losing one's life for a material thing? He would reserve judgment on her father.

"Why did he think the coins are in Crossroads Bay?"

"Pop found documentation at the maritime museum chronicling the Drake family voyages. The coins were also mentioned in a few of the many journals he had found." Her passion translated to her cheeks as they flushed a pretty pink. "Looking for the code word *Inheritance*, he found several entries, some as simple as, 'I tucked The Inheritance in my belt and we set sail.' Once they made it to Hawaii in the eighteenth century, all mention of them ceased. We figured they stayed in one family, or at least in one place for another two hundred years."

"So do you mind me asking how your dad's death is tied to these coins?"

Meranda winced. "I'm sorry you had to hear about that at the party." She drew in a breath. "You know about the shipwreck off our coast."

"A little. We learned about it in school."

"My great-great-grandfather built that ship, and then later the lighthouse."

"Wait." He pressed his finger to his temple. "His name was. . ."

"Augustus Drake. He was on his way back from Hawaii after his older brother died, and he ran into a storm. The crippled boat never made it to shore."

"Older brother. So you believe the coins passed to Augustus after his brother died."

She nodded. "I have confirmation. He'd written some letters to a sister in San Francisco. In one he said The Inheritance was where no one would find it. And that's why we believed they were in the shipwreck." Her gaze drifted to the horizon. His followed as well to see the gentle glow from the sun's rays give their final efforts before night swallowed them completely. Then, in a barely audible voice, Meranda spoke. "Pop had gotten trapped in the shipwreck and ran out of air."

Paul set the mop aside and knelt in front of Meranda, taking her hands in his own. "I'm so sorry for your loss."

She gripped his fingers and closed her eyes. He had the feeling she wasn't a crier, but a small tear slipped from the inside corner of her right eye. With a quick swipe of her hand, it was gone. When she focused on him once more, it was with clear eyes, and he knew the door into her grief had closed to him. But he thanked God for the brief glimpse he'd had inside. Now he knew better how to pray for her.

"Sun's down." She gingerly stood, testing her footing with her new injury. "I need to rinse the deck." She limped to where she'd draped the hose over the railing. "You might want to stand behind me."

Over the spraying water, Paul continued the discussion. He still wasn't clear on a few things. "Your father thought the coins were in the shipwreck. Why do you believe they're in the lighthouse?"

She spoke over her shoulder. "Pop and I dove the wreck several times. He hired a professional crew. To me it stands to reason that if we didn't find them after all our dives, they would be in the lighthouse. And recently I found a letter that confirms it—sort of."

"Sort of."

"It doesn't say where the coins are, just that they're safe."

"Could be they're safely buried deep in the hull of the sunken ship."

Meranda turned around, an exasperated expression on her face. Was she contemplating using the hose to rinse him off the boat? "Now you're confusing the issue. I just had my mind made up."

"Sorry." He tried his most charming smile, the one that kept him off the hook with Abuelita.

She shrugged. "It's okay. I'll concentrate on the lighthouse for now. Hopefully I'm on the right path."

"Sounds like a good plan."

Meranda grinned back, then quickly finished her chore. She excused herself to stow the cleaning supplies below and lock up. Paul stepped to the dock and coiled up the hose for her. While waiting, he allowed all he had learned about her to sink in. He had thought the beautiful captain a fascinating woman before learning her history. But now—oh, man, another thought hit him. When she returned from below with her canvas bag slung on her shoulder, he asked, "Were you with your dad on that last dive?"

"No." The light went out in her eyes.

Water gently slapped the boat. Screeching seagulls glided high in the sky. Voices from the other boaters drifted by.

But Meranda was silent.

❧

The bruise on Meranda's hip throbbed like crazy, but it didn't hurt nearly as bad as her answer to Paul's question. No, she hadn't gone with her father.

She felt like a wimp as Paul helped her negotiate from the boat to the dock. Their footsteps played a wooden drumbeat as he came up beside her. Meranda cast a sidelong gaze at him. "Are you working tonight?"

"No. Monday is my day off from the restaurant, and I have no catering jobs this evening." He slipped his hands into his pockets. "You wouldn't want to get a bite to eat, would you?"

That's what she was going to ask. "I know a good place for paella, but I hear the chef is off on Mondays."

"Yeah. Too bad." He chuckled. "There's a little café not far from here, though. No Spanish foods, but the hamburgers are the best in town."

She pinched at her shirt. "I've been on a fishing trip. Even though Ethan did all the work, I'm not exactly fresh."

He gave her a brisk one-armed hug. "You're fine, and this place isn't fancy."

She may not have smelled great, but he smelled amazing. A girlie sense of enjoyment shot through her as she realized his mouth was about eye level. "Okay. I'll follow you."

Just a couple of blocks from the wharf, Paul pulled his hybrid into a small parking lot and Meranda parked her truck beside him. This was the touristy part of town, with gray-planked buildings and short timber posts with rope for fencing—all ambience to simulate Crossroads Bay a century ago. In a couple of months, the town would be teeming with visitors, but for now only a smattering of people wandered the boardwalks.

They entered the restaurant through a screen door and seated themselves at a wooden table shellacked to a waterproof shine. Paper placemats advertised the place—Capt. Tony's—and a peg-leg pirate logo greeted them with a salute.

"I've never eaten here before." Meranda's mouth watered as the smell of grilled meat drifted from the kitchen. With eager fingers, she pulled two vinyl menus from behind the salt and pepper shakers and handed one to Paul.

"They have good fish sandwiches, too, but I come here for the cheeseburgers."

"That's odd."

"Why?"

"You're a gourmet chef. Why would you come to a dive for hamburgers?"

The waitress came to take their drink orders, never indicating she'd heard Meranda say the word *dive*, then left with promises to return shortly after they'd looked at the menus.

Paul leaned in and with a conspiratorial whisper said, "I'm thinking of stealing the cook." He then placed his index finger to his lips.

Meranda put her forearm on the table and also leaned in. "Doing some pirating of your own?"

"You could put it that way." He winked. "This guy is a genius with food."

The waitress returned and took their orders of two cheeseburgers, coleslaw, and fries.

After an awkward silence, neither apparently knowing where to begin the conversation, Meranda finally opened a topic. "You know my story. What's yours?"

He tossed his head back and chuckled. "Ah. Where do I begin?"

"The beginning?" She took a sip of her soda.

"Okay. I was born here, in Crossroads Bay."

"Well, we have that in common."

"I was raised by a single mom and my grandparents. I never knew my dad. He died when I was a baby."

"Oh, I'm sorry."

"We managed okay." He shrugged. "We worked in the restaurant."

"Even you? As a little boy?"

"Well, no. As a little boy I played under the tables with my cousins and made Abuelita, my grandmother, angry." His smile told her he'd had a good childhood. "As I grew older, I took an interest in the kitchen. Then, a few years ago, I lost my mother." He tapped his fork on the table, a staccato rhythm that no doubt echoed his broken heart. "I was twenty-three."

So they both had endured loss. Meranda fiddled with her napkin. She ached for him. Losing a parent hurt like a harpoon to the chest. She wouldn't wish that on anybody, but especially not on a warm, gentle soul like Paul.

"My aunt and uncle needed someone to help on their alpaca ranch, so I moved there until a year ago. My grandmother called to tell me she wanted to retire from the restaurant, so I came back home."

"But you're a caterer. Do you run the restaurant, too?"

"No, when I got back here and discussed everything with Abuelita—"

"Excuse me, why do you call her Abuelita?"

He grinned. "It's Spanish for 'grandma' or 'granny.' Less formal than *abuela*, or 'grandmother.'"

"I look forward to meeting your abuelita."

Color leaped to his cheeks. Had she embarrassed him by suggesting she'd like to meet his family?

"Anyway," he continued, "I told her my real love is catering. I get pleasure out of helping people make their special day. . .

well. . .special. I'm not confined to the restaurant, and I get to meet and interact with customers. My cousin Al also grew up working in the restaurant. So we comanage—he's responsible for the restaurant, and I do the catering."

"So that's something else we have in common."

He arched his eyebrow.

"We both went into the family business."

His smile came easily and reached deep into his eyes. "Yes, we did."

Their meal came, and Meranda had to agree that her cheeseburger was extraordinary. Juicy and full of flavor.

Paul rolled it around in his mouth, as if tasting fine wine. "Mm-hm." He nodded and pulled a small notebook from his pocket. "Sour cream."

"He puts sour cream in his hamburgers? How could you tell that with one bite?"

She bit into hers as he did, nabbing only the meat. As it rolled on her tongue, she tried to concentrate on the individual tastes of everything that went into the meat. She nodded. "Mm-hm." Then, "Uh-uh. All I taste is really good meat."

He laughed. "It takes practice."

As she munched, she searched her mind for something else to talk about. Naturally her mind settled on Paul's enigma. "Let's talk about your aversion to boats. I think I can help you overcome that."

The grin on his lips fell, and his face blanched. She hoped she hadn't ruined his meal.

"How?"

"Meet me at the dock next Monday morning, and I'll show you."

When he hesitated to agree, she reached out to still his fork playing staccato. "Trust me?"

His hand quieted, and he turned his deep brown eyes to her. "Yes."

six

Monday morning Meranda hopped out of bed with more energy than she'd had in a long time. The plan she had hatched the other night to get him back on her boat spun in her mind. Would Paul go for it? Or would he back out at the last minute?

They had spoken on the phone nearly every night the past week. But no matter how much he begged, she wouldn't spill what she had in mind to help him get over his fear of boats.

As she dressed she opted for deck shoes instead of her tall rubber-soled black boots, which were reserved for work.

As she finger-combed her hair, it fought for control as always. She finally made it submit to a tight rubber band, but when she grabbed her scarf and started to tie it over her head, she stopped when she saw herself in the mirror. Shades of her sisters morphed from her image in a family resemblance, but she would never be as pretty as either of them. Rose resembled her name, soft pink features on a flawless face. Julianne's freshness was what made her special. Bright eyes, ready smile. Meranda's big bones and height kept her from feeling feminine.

The scarf still lay in her hand. She folded it into a thin strip, removed the rubber band, and shook out her hair, then used the scarf as a headband, allowing her hair to flow down her back. She turned her head from side to side to see the effect. The soft hair bordering her face helped to round out her features. She sucked in a breath. That was Mom staring back at her in the mirror. The mom she remembered as a child. When they were all happy.

She backed away from the mirror.

On the way through the house, she grabbed a jacket and a cooler full of food and drinks, then got into her pickup and drove to the dock.

When she arrived, Paul was waiting in his car for her. Butterflies warred with the minnows in her stomach as he got out and ambled to her pickup. She hopped out and reached for the cooler in the bed.

"Let me carry that." He grabbed the handle.

She found herself blushing—blushing!—as he seemed to notice her hair. He smiled, and her hand maddeningly reached up to finger a curl in an uncharacteristic flirty movement. *Blast!*

As they headed toward the dock, he asked, "How's your pride?"

"Huh?" Oh, the spill she took the other day. She rubbed her hip. "Much better, thank you. The ice kept the swelling down."

As they strolled, he stopped at the charter boat, but she kept going, ignoring his hesitation. His steps hustled behind her—a brisk clapping on the boards.

"Um. . .where are we going?"

She continued to walk on the pier until she reached the smaller boat slips. "Here." She swept her hand toward the twenty-five-foot cruiser. "This is my boat."

His brow furrowed, and his gaze swung back to the larger charter. "I thought that was your boat."

"They both are. My father gave this one to all of us girls. But my sisters never showed much interest, so it's virtually mine." In fact, the other two had been on the boat only a handful of times in the past year.

He glanced at the name painted on the side. "The *Romanda Jule.* I get it. Rose, Meranda, and Julianne." His gaze fell to the cooler at her feet. "Do you think I'm getting on that boat? It's a lot smaller than the other one."

"The way you leaped onto my boat the other day tells me you're trainable."

"Well, it's one thing to be brave when tied to a dock. Quite another out in the open ocean."

"So let's try the open ocean."

Paul didn't budge.

"I'm serious. The only way to get over your fear is to face it."

"I did face it, remember? I spent the entire cruise buckled over."

She refused to let that be his last experience on a boat. "So, are you afraid, or do you just get seasick?"

"I'm afraid of getting seasick."

"Okay." She rummaged in her bag. After drawing out the palm-sized plastic box, she handed it to him. "This will help the nausea."

He opened the box. "Wristbands? Am I going jogging?"

She lifted one and turned it inside out. "See the plastic bead? Situate this where it causes a pressure point on your vein. Like this." She helped him place both bands correctly. "It's the same thing I did to your wrists that first day when you catered on my boat. So," she slipped her hand around his elbow, "are you coming?"

The dock seemed to capture Paul's shoes, preventing him from moving forward.

She leaped from the dock to the boat and placed her fists on her hips. "Do I have to fall again to get you to come on board?"

"No." He gingerly moved from the dock to the back platform and finally made it on deck. "And don't fall while we're out in the middle of nowhere, either. I wouldn't know how to get us back."

"And that, my fine gentleman, is what I'm going to teach you today." She waved him to the helm.

"Seriously?"

"Yep. You're going to drive my boat."

"Cool."

❧

Paul sat in the passenger seat, paying close attention to everything Meranda did as she motored the boat away from the dock—although her hair distracted him. His fingers ached to touch the soft curls.

"I've heard," she said as she grabbed the throttle and eased away from the dock, "that a good way to avoid seasickness is to steer the boat. I don't know if it's because you feel more in control or because you're concentrating on something other than nausea."

It didn't matter to Paul what the reasons were. He was willing to try anything to keep from looking like a fool again.

Once they were in open water, she slowed down and cut the engine. Then she stood, and he slipped into the captain's seat.

She patted his shoulder. "You okay there, skipper?"

"A little nervous still. But what man wouldn't want the chance to drive a boat on the open sea?" And have the chance to redeem himself in the eyes of the beautiful captain?

After she showed him the first thing he needed to know, how to radio the coast guard, she tutored him on how to start the boat, accelerate, and slow down. Paul eased into an enjoyable clip, pushing the speed slightly as he felt more comfortable. Invigorating chilly air wrapped around the vessel, but his adrenaline warmed him.

"What do you think?" Meranda asked him from the chair to his left.

"The wristbands are working. . . . Without the nausea, I think I like this." As he opened up the throttle, he didn't know what was more thrilling—the speed or this beautiful woman sitting in close proximity as she coached him.

"It handles much easier than I expected."

"And how do you feel?"

"Great! It must have been a matter of control. The more I learn about the boat, the more confident I am on the water."

She checked the bearings and asked him to slow down. "Here—this is where I wanted to take you. See that buoy floating in the water? Head toward it."

After killing the engine, they drifted near the buoy. She stood and motioned for him to follow her. They moved to the back of the boat into the warming sunlight where rays painted golds and reds in the strands of her hair. She pulled her jacket around her as the slight breeze blew moist air from the north. Should he rub her arms, warm her?

"This is where it happened." She pointed to the water below the boat.

He glanced around at the open sea, the shore several miles in the distance. "The shipwreck?"

She nodded. "This is where my dad died."

This time he couldn't stop himself from offering comfort by caressing her upper arms. She leaned back against him, and he prayed his presence would console her. "Do you know what happened?"

She shrugged. "All I know is what the report said. He was in Augustus's cabin. Pop had gotten a plan of the ship and a ledger, so we knew exactly where to look."

"You mean the ship is intact down there?" He looked at the water wishing he had special powers to see it without diving. "I figured it was in several pieces."

She pulled away and turned to rest against the rail. "Remember the *Titanic*, how she broke in two?"

He nodded.

"The part that had filled with water is still pretty much whole. That's how they've found so many artifacts. The other half had air still in most of the ship. When it hit bottom, it exploded from the pressure of releasing all that air. This ship," she pointed to the waves, "filled with water slowly. The crew tried their best to get her to shore, but she had nothing left to give. When she sank, she was like a waterlogged toy and drifted to the bottom."

Paul had to admit he knew nothing about shipwrecks. "I'm confused. If I knew about this shipwreck, I'm sure your dad did. Why did it take him so long to look for it?"

"For one, he didn't have the means." She held up her fingers. "For two, the *Victoria Jane* had been buried for almost a hundred years. He had scuba dived the area looking for a hint most of his adult life, but it wasn't until the big earthquake a decade ago that her bell was unearthed. He found that and knew the ship was under the sand there someplace."

"Oh, so after that, he was finally able to get some funding to dig her out."

She nodded. "He hired a team to dive it before anyone else could get down there and claim the coins. The salvage crew sucked the sand off with an underwater vacuum cleaner called an air lift. They managed to get most of the deck and about a third of the bow cleared so they could go inside the ship. It took them several futile tries, but the *Victoria Jane* wouldn't give up her secrets easily."

"So they didn't find anything."

"Actually, they found plenty of things. The ship's bell, articles from the cabins, the dishes they used. These things are all in the museum now. But no coins. Pop obtained a sketch from the shipbuilding company and learned where Augustus's quarters were. It was tough figuring out the ship since part of it has been claimed by the ocean floor, but eventually he was able to find the cabin. He concentrated his efforts there, but died before he could finish."

"What happened that day?" Paul reached out and stroked

her arm, letting her know he was there for support.

"Pop and Phil—did Jessie tell you about her dad's connection to mine?"

He nodded.

"They were in Augustus's cabin. They had tied off a nylon line so they could follow it out when they were ready. According to Phil, they were done, and he swam out of the cabin first when something fell off the ship that created a silt storm. Visibility zero." She held up her hand, creating an *O* with her fingers. "He continued on, thinking Pop was behind him. But when he surfaced, Pop didn't. Knowing Pop had little air left, he grabbed a couple of fresh tanks from the third man on the dive boat and told him to call the coast guard. By the time he got to Pop, it was too late. The line had broken and wrapped around Pop's legs. It looked like he'd tried to cut himself free, but he'd run out of air."

Her eyes grew even sadder, if that were possible. "I wish I'd been with him that day."

"What could you have done? You'd only have put yourself in danger."

She shrugged one shoulder. "At least he wouldn't have been alone."

They stood a few moments longer paying their silent respects. Finally she offered a brave smile. "Enough of that. I just wanted you to see why finding the coins is so important to me." She pushed away from the rail. "And now I'd like to show you something else."

Back in the captain's seat, Meranda urged Paul to hang on. She opened the throttle, and they bounced along at a thrilling clip. Paul gripped the railing near him. His fear barometer raised slightly, but nothing he couldn't handle. He concentrated on the exhilarating feel of the wind on his face, the g-force against his skin, and the amazing woman by his side.

After shooting across the surface for what must've been a couple dozen miles, Meranda slowed the boat to a putter. "Isn't the coast beautiful from out here?"

He tore his gaze from her and found the view breathtaking. Green hillsides huddled to the water's edge with occasional beaches in varying hues of dark and milk chocolate separating them. Large sea stacks rose from the water, rock formations that he'd seen shoreside but never from this angle. They drifted by Face Rock off Bandon Beach. It didn't look like a face on this side.

Within an hour, they'd made it all the way down to Gold Beach. Rogue Reef, a small island mound nearly three miles offshore, came into view.

Meranda cut the engine. "Listen. Do you hear it?"

Paul nodded. Two thousand harbor and steller seals barked a cacophonous concert as they sunbathed and played on the reef. He also smelled the banquet of rotting fish for two thousand guests. Thankfully, the seasick bands on his wrists were working to disable the trigger. "On shore this just looks like a big rock, but from here it looks alive." Hundreds of blubbery necks swayed and jerked, creating an eerie Medusa-like effect.

"We're about a quarter-mile from the reef." She opened a compartment under the console and brought out a set of binoculars. "Here, use these. This is a view you'd never get from shore, unless of course you've got some high-powered specs."

He placed the binoculars to his eyes and focused using the wheel on top. They immediately put him in the middle of the seal party. "Wow. I can see their faces."

She pointed to the north of the island where two seals were body surfing. "Now that looks like fun."

"Hey! Surf's up, dude! Wouldn't it be nice to be that carefree?" No grandmother looking over his shoulder, no catering dramas between mothers and daughters. Just a day of surfing. With Meranda. That would be like a three-course meal with crema catalana for dessert—very nice.

While they drifted, enjoying the remarkably serene chaos, Meranda stood. "I brought food. Are you hungry?"

Paul groaned. "You brought food? Did you cook it yourself?"

She cuffed his shoulder playfully. "I may not be a gourmet cook, but I know how to slap together a sandwich."

"Operative word: slap."

As she went below to the small galley, her voice drifted from the steps. "I think I'm very brave to fix you a meal. Especially after the fiasco at my mother's house the other night."

"What fiasco? You held your own with your sister's cooking class."

"Thanks. I just know that I'll never be as domestic as Mom or Rose." She brought out sandwich bags and cold sodas.

"And no one expects you to be. You have your own gifts."

She tilted her head. "Tell that to my mother."

As he opened the cellophane bag just enough so the ham and cheese sandwich peeked out, he continued. "I apologize for teasing you. Believe me, I'm appreciative that you thought of lunch. I'm starving." He took a bite, then pretended to choke and received another thump on his shoulder—an action negated by the smile on her face.

Although the nippy air tingled his skin, he found himself quite comfortable. It could have been the company. Or it could have been God smiling down on him. Whatever the case, he knew there was nowhere else in the world he'd rather be than floating in the Pacific Ocean with Meranda Drake.

While they ate, Meranda pulled a small envelope out of her bag. "I brought something to show you. Please be careful that the wind doesn't blow this away. It's the letter I told you about."

He opened it and saw it was from Augustus to his sister. He read aloud. " 'As you know, with the untimely demise of our brother, I became the keeper of The Inheritance.' " He stopped and raised his eyebrow. Seeing the word in a historic missive made it all the more real. He continued to read. " 'I brought it back from Hawaii with me and want you to know that it is safe, and I'm concretely sure it is where no one will find it.' " He whistled and handed it back to her. "This sure looks like The Inheritance is real and apparently somewhere close."

"Now I'm sure it's in the lighthouse. It would be a perfect place. Look at the word *concretely*. The lighthouse is a solid structure of brick and cement. I think that's a clue." She slipped the letter back in the bag. "You want to see what the coins look like?"

"Sure."

She unhooked a chain from around her neck and drew out a circular object from her shirt. When she placed it into his palm, he drew in a quick breath. "Wow."

"This pendant was my dad's, handed down from Augustus to Grandpa to Pop. We found pictures of the coins on the Internet and"—she pointed to the front of the pendant, a little larger than a minted half dollar—"this insignia is an exact replica of one side of the coins. Probably cast from the original. We think it had been made to tie the coins back to us if they were ever lost or stolen."

The image in the center was of two pillars with waves rising between them. On the back of the pendant he found an inscription, worn but readable. "JG.IG. What does it mean?"

"I don't know. The pendant wasn't mentioned in our research."

He shook his head. "I don't remember reading any of this in my history books."

"Which is why everyone thinks they're a myth. But my father found documentation. Captains' logs, letters to relatives.

The coins do exist, and this pendant is proof." Her eyes flashed hot. "Pop was the last male Drake. I need to find them for him. Now do you see why your help is so important?"

"I do." He scratched his chin. "I can still only promise to keep my eyes open. Please understand that I can't risk angering a client by getting caught where I'm not supposed to be. They let us into their homes in full faith that we won't disturb anything. I have a code of honor that not only comes from my profession but also from my God."

Her mouth pulled to one side. "I understand."

But did she? And why did the passion in her eyes die when he mentioned God?

seven

As the lighthouse wedding drew near, Meranda decided she was asking too much of Paul. Maybe she should try to convince the owner to allow her in once more.

She drove up to the dreaded iron gate. If she ever got the land back, that would be the first thing to go. She left her truck and found an intercom box mounted to the fence made of solid black bars. Her trembling finger found the buzzer. The speaker grid on the intercom reminded her of an open O-shaped mouth—as in the word *no*.

"Hello. Who is it?" The male voice barked like a guard dog.

"Meranda Drake. May I speak to Judge Bernard?"

"This is he."

"I don't know if you remember me. I'm Gilbert Drake's daughter. Our ancestor built the lighthouse."

Silence. Had he hung up? Was he coming to the gate to talk to her in person? She continued on, hoping he could still hear her. "Since you're back in Crossroads Bay for your daughter's wedding, I was wondering if I might visit. I just want to see the lighthouse that my great-great-grandfather built."

The speaker crackled the judge's reply. "I'd like to indulge you, Miss Drake, but as you can imagine, there is a lot going on over here. Good day."

"Wait!" She gritted her teeth but tried to sound amiable. "I understand. I promise I won't bother anyone. You won't even know I'm there."

"Look. I'm sure you were able to play here with the previous owner's permission, but I don't have time for this.

It's our lighthouse now, and we don't welcome strangers." A click ended the conversation.

Play? Is that what he thought she wanted to do? And no, she'd never been in the lighthouse because of jerks like this guy who wouldn't allow it. *Beelzebub himself could hardly desire better company.*

She stormed back to her truck and turned around. On the way to the main road, she turned right into Lighthouse View Park. Another car sat in the lot, and a family ate lunch at one of the two picnic tables. The viewing area, a knob of land above a cliff, beckoned her as it often did when she needed to feel close to the lighthouse. Pebbles on the short path crunched under her feet, and she stopped at the three-foot rock wall. A flat cement layer on top of the thick wall created a bench. She sat down, faced the lighthouse, and pulled her knees to her chin. The tall white structure stood proud on the point.

"I don't know what else to do, Pop. Other than scale the gate and trespass, I think this door is closed to us."

A movement on the road caught her eye, and a black, decadent-looking sedan sped away from the property and past the park. The blue book value on the vehicle would probably feed a small country.

Was that the judge? Would there be someone else who might let her in? Meranda regarded the lighthouse and winked. There was more than one way to scale a fish.

She hustled back to her truck and rummaged around in her diver bag behind the seat. Among the accessories she used while diving, her hand grasped her underwater digital camera.

Back at the gate, she pressed the buzzer again. Perhaps she'd have better luck with the wife.

Thankfully, a female voice answered.

"Mrs. Bernard?"

"Mrs. Bernard passed away several years ago. I'm Glenys Bernard, one of the daughters. To whom am I speaking?"

"I'm sorry for your loss." If the judge had lost someone he loved, wouldn't he understand her situation? "This is. . .Judith Francis, reporter for the *Crossroads Bay Examiner*." Meranda had to squeeze the lie through her teeth. Pop had raised her to never deceive, but maybe just this once. . .

"How may I help you?"

Meranda quelled her excitement over the cordial greeting. "I understand your sister is getting married. May I interview her for our. . ." What was it called? "Oh, our society page." Smooth. Better keep the day job.

"Well. . .my sister isn't here yet. She and her fiancé will be arriving in a few days. But I'd be happy to grant you an interview."

Meranda fought to maintain a professional tone. But she hopped on her toes as the anticipation gurgled inside her like a fountain. Hopefully there were no cameras.

Just as the gate began to slide open, the black sedan returned.

Blast! Had the judge forgotten something?

The car rolled to a stop behind her truck, and the driver's window lowered. A portly man with thinning gray-dappled hair stuck his head out the window. "May I help you?"

She cleared her throat. Time for Captain Ahab to confront Moby Dick. As she passed her truck's open driver door, she snatched the camera for effect and walked to the black car. "Judge Bernard?"

He nodded.

"I'm Judith Francis, reporter for the *Crossroads Bay Examiner*."

A pause. "Never heard of you."

"I've come to interview you on your daughter's wedding."

"No interviews." He backed up and positioned the car to go around Meranda's truck.

She couldn't let him go. "But I just spoke to your daughter about the wedding."

The car stopped. "Alison?"

"No, sir. Your other daughter, Glenys. I told her I'd love to interview the family."

He sat back into his seat and rubbed his face. A frustrated father sigh emitted from his lips. "What did she tell you?"

"That she'd grant an interview. She seemed quite excited."

"She's an actress." The word sounded as if he'd said *cockroach*. "She was probably thrilled to get some publicity, even if it's through her sister."

"Since I'm here, may I talk to Glenys?"

The car started rolling again. "Glenys or Alison, it doesn't matter. We don't need reporters hanging around. Good day."

"Wait!" She was beginning to feel more like paparazzo than a reporter, of which she was neither.

He stopped again and thrust his head out the window. "You sound familiar. Are you that Drake person who was here not even an hour ago?"

Oh, why didn't she disguise her voice? The lie hovered on her lips, but try as she might, she could not deny she was a Drake.

He took her hesitancy as a confession. "I suggest you go home, Miss Drake, before I call the authorities." His head disappeared back into the car, and the window rose like a shield. After passing through the gate, it clanked shut, finalizing his answer.

Anger surged through her. She deserved to see that lighthouse.

❧

The week of the lighthouse wedding, Paul had chosen staff from the restaurant to help. Now, the morning of, they bustled back and forth loading the two vans. He stood just outside the restaurant, the morning sun burning away the fog, as he checked off items.

"Pablo." His abuelita stood behind him, about elbow height.

"What do you think, Abuelita? This could be an important account. I hear the judge holds many social gatherings whenever he visits for the summer." And the judge had told him he, too, had been partial to Philippe, the deported French caterer. How great would it be to get all his disgruntled clients?

"It is good." Her wrinkled smile pleased Paul. "Would you like me to come?"

"No!" He squeezed his eyes shut and prayed for God to temper his tongue. "I mean, it's not necessary. You'd be on your feet all day."

"Pshhh!" Her way of saying tsk-tsk. *"¿De veras?"*

"Yes, really."

"Your abuelo and I built this restaurant."

"I know, Abuelita."

"From the ground up."

"I know, Abuelita."

"We bring our family's food to this country." She held out her palms, arthritic fingers like sticks trying to flex into sad little fists. "With these two hands."

"I know. And now it's time for you to rest and let Albert and me work for a change. Eh?" He kissed her forehead and pointed her toward the building. "I've got this under control."

"Pshhh!"

He shook his head at her retreating figure. The black and gray bun bobbed with the vitality of a teenager's ponytail.

Presently, he returned to the kitchen with his clipboard and checked off all the food they would be taking. Jessie had disappeared, and he needed her to supervise the equipment. Derrick, Jessie's boyfriend and a member of Paul's staff, walked into the kitchen for another load.

Paul pointed his pen at him. "Have you seen Jessie?"

"Uh, yeah. She's on her cell phone talking to Meranda, I think."

Meranda. Those two were getting thicker than his bouil-
labaisse. Were they up to something?

He hadn't initiated contact with Meranda since their day
on the water. He sensed she wasn't a Christian, and he needed
to pray about his growing affection for her. But she and Jessie
had hit it off—their fathers and love of the ocean common
denominators.

After the two vehicles were loaded, he gathered his team,
including Jessie, for a pep talk.

"This is going to be a big party. Are you all up to the
challenge?" They nodded. "Jessie, where is the sixth server?"

"She called in sick. I found a replacement and will pick her
up on the way."

He'd have to be satisfied with that.

"You all know your stations, right?" he continued. "If you
need anything, be sure to let either Jess or I know. And
remember," he addressed Jessie more than the others, "the
kitchen and back patio are the only places we're allowed to
go. No wandering. We aren't guests."

He and three of the waitstaff piled into the larger van. He
looked in the rearview mirror as Jessie and Derrick pulled
in line behind him. He lost them a few blocks later, and he
assumed she had turned off to get the substitute server.
Traffic thickened as they drove through town. Although
tourist season didn't officially kick off for another month, the
warm, dry weather this last week of April brought out the
locals, who no doubt feared the sunshine wouldn't last.

The road he sought appeared, and he turned. Jessie hadn't
caught up, but she knew the way. He meandered up the little
paved road through grassy meadows until he came to a gate.
He waited there for Jessie before alerting the house of their
presence.

When she pulled up behind him, he got out and buzzed
the intercom at the gate, then identified himself. The gate

opened, and they both drove forward. The road broke into a *V*, the left heading toward the lighthouse and the right toward the dwelling. He took the right fork and after a quarter of a mile pulled toward the back of the house to unload the van.

Judge Bernard met him and started barking orders. This gave Paul no chance to breathe or meet the new member of the staff. He'd have to trust that Jessie oriented her.

Everyone bustled about, their white shirts and black slacks looking crisp and clean. He puffed with pride as he watched five people working like busy ants. He glanced around. Where was the sixth?

Finally, he spotted her behind the van and gazing at the lighthouse. This wouldn't do. He walked up behind her and tapped her shoulder. She swung around and gasped. Gray eyes blinked at him from behind black-framed glasses, and she adjusted a dark wig.

"Meranda?" Why hadn't he recognized that leggy five-foot-nine stature? "What do you think you're doing?"

She peeked at him over the glasses but apparently had no excuse ready.

"Jessica!" His gaze searched the grounds for the commander of this operation.

Paul seized Meranda's elbow and led her to the patio. Her accomplice poked her head out the door. "Yes, boss?" When she saw Meranda standing next to him, she disappeared back into the kitchen.

Paul, not to be ignored, grabbed Meranda's hand and dragged her into the house. He prayed the whole way that the family was too busy to hear the conversation he was about to have.

"Jessie." He hissed at her back as she stood at the sink.

She turned innocent, round eyes on him. "Yes, boss?"

He thrust a pointing finger toward Meranda. "What is the meaning of this?"

Meranda stepped between them. "Don't blame Jessie. It was my idea."

&a·

Meranda stood her ground as Paul turned an angry glare on her. He had been her last hope to get into the lighthouse, and she wouldn't back down now.

"What part of 'no, it would hurt my business' did you not understand?"

"I'm sorry, Paul, but—"

He held up his hand. "Don't." He took a deep breath, no doubt calming himself to temper his words. "I should have someone drive you back, but they're all needed here." He looked at Jessie. "What happened to the sixth server?"

Jessie spoke without flinching. "She really did call in sick this morning." She glanced down at the ceramic floor tiles. "Meranda's protecting me. It was my idea to call her and give her the opportunity to come along. She didn't know I hadn't told you until we got here."

While this was the truth, Meranda's stomach felt queasy knowing she should have come clean with Paul. She dropped her gaze to his shoes. "I'm sorry."

"Are you?" He placed his hands on his hips. "You could have told me right away instead of sneaking around. I'm not happy, but I don't mind putting you to work."

She straightened and looked him in the eye. "I guess I handled the whole thing poorly. I'm sorry. It just felt great to get past the gate. I tried talking to the owner, but he flatly refused me after I told him who I was."

"He's a judge. He presided over some high-profile cases this last year. Of course he's cautious."

He was downright rude, actually. "I understand if you want to send me away. But if you let me stay, I'll pull my own weight. And you don't even have to pay me."

"I'm not condoning this at all, but. . .you can stay." Meranda's heart flipped in her chest. "However, you will not go into the lighthouse." He glowered at his assistant. "She's your responsibility. If she breaks, spills, or otherwise embarrasses this company, it's on your head."

"Yes, bo. . .sir."

"Thank you, Paul." Meranda vowed never to involve Paul against his wishes again. But she was grateful for his mercy.

Paul started to walk away, but threw one last parting shot. "And take off that ridiculous wig and glasses."

Her hands flew to the stiff wig that Jessie had lent her. "I can't. The judge will recognize me."

Paul pinched the bridge of his nose and left without another word.

۞

Less than an hour later, Paul looked out onto the lawn where his crew had dressed the tables with linens, sparkling china, and crystal goblets. Up the hill, two young men in suits, perhaps in their early twenties, directed elegantly dressed guests toward the 150 white chairs facing the ocean between the lighthouse and a pair of pillars.

He had a moment to breathe before the reception and a moment to say a brief prayer for Meranda. It wasn't fair that she had to resort to trickery just to see the lighthouse.

But Jessie! What had she been thinking? They were going to discuss this, and he had to think hard on whether he should fire her. He could only assume her fast friendship with Meranda had caused the lapse in judgment.

As the minister stepped into place and the music started, Paul positioned the waitstaff to be ready to serve. Judge Bernard had told him the ceremony would be brief. Meranda stood with Jessie. His neck tensed up, and he pulled his head to one side to crack it.

A flash near Meranda caught his eye. Fire leapt from her sleeve, and Jessie grabbed a towel to douse it. He ran over.

"What happened?" The burning smell of cotton invaded his nose.

"My fault," Meranda said. "I got too close to the Sterno can."

"Did you burn yourself?" His heart thumped hard in his chest at the thought she might be hurt. He inspected her arm where the flame had chewed a dark jagged hole into her white cuff.

"No, it just singed my blouse."

"And maybe some hair. Go to the kitchen and run some cool water on your hand."

"I'm fine."

He glared at her, and she obeyed. Where could he put her where she wouldn't hurt herself or others?

Finally, he stationed Meranda at the three-tiered wedding cake. "Don't cut any of it until the bride and groom get their first piece."

"I know how it works." She frowned, clearly miffed.

"Actually, don't touch anything. Derrick here will cut the cake. If you're good, I might let you serve the tables."

A swift breeze suddenly blew in from the ocean, catching a woman's hat in the back row of the ceremony. Paul ran to catch it as it tumbled on its wide brim like an errant tire on the highway. He snatched the sunny yellow hat before it found its way to the dirt road. With his heart palpitating from the exercise, he ran back to the grateful elderly woman.

He backed away from the guests and waited in the shadow of the lighthouse to catch his breath. He contemplated slipping inside, but after his lectures on the evils of sneaking around, he felt that might be inappropriate. Instead, he watched the end of the ceremony as his heart settled to a normal rhythm.

The minister and the couple stood between the two white pillars. He had thought the wedding planner had provided the seven-foot-tall posts—an intricate carving in the tops of each looked like castle rooks—and inwardly applauded her for finding some that were so realistic. But when the couple said "I do" and the wedding party moved, he could see the pillars were a permanent structure marking a path to the beach.

Wait a minute.

He hustled back to the patio, adrenaline now pumping his overtaxed heart. He told everyone to man their stations as the ceremony was over, and he grabbed Meranda's arm to pull her out of earshot from Derrick. "Do you have the necklace you showed me the other day?" His fingers formed a circle. "The big one." He wanted her to hurry before the guests started meandering toward the patio.

She pulled on the chain around her neck and drew it out.

"Look at the pendant and look at where the couple was standing."

Her gaze went from the pendant to the pillars and back. Her eyes widened as she focused on Paul. "It's them. The pillars on my pendant." She slapped her own forehead. "I thought they were just posts marking the stairs to the beach. Even in the pictures I've seen, they never seemed to resemble the pendant."

"From where I was standing directly behind the lighthouse, I saw this scene." He tapped the insignia. "Are they there as a clue?"

All she seemed to be able to do was smile.

Paul wrapped his hand around hers as they clutched the necklace. "We have to get you into that lighthouse."

eight

Meranda would not have hurt Paul's business for the world. She'd been foolish to sneak onto the property.

But she was here now, and Paul finally seemed to have caught the vision.

Thankfully, they didn't have to scheme their way into the lighthouse. After the cutting of the cake, Judge Bernard made an announcement. "Anyone wishing to tour the lighthouse may do so now."

Paul's arm shot straight up. "Does that include the staff, sir?"

"Absolutely! The more the merrier I always say." Apparently social gatherings softened up the judge.

Meranda wanted to spring across the patio and lay a kiss on Paul. But she caught his eye and mouthed a thank-you instead. When he winked back, she felt as though her feet lifted off the ground. Jessie may have been her cohort in crime, but this man was stealthily stealing her heart.

Paul gathered his employees together. "Okay, it will be a little while yet. Once they get to the dessert, we won't be needed as heavily."

Jessie patted Meranda on the back and whispered, "We did it."

Yes, they did, but her conscience still niggled at her. Paul did it right and asked permission, although she had tried that and gotten shot down for her efforts. She heaved a huge sigh as she scraped dishes. However it happened, she was here now and about to touch a piece of her ancestors' history.

The house had belonged to Augustus, but the historic

part of the structure was off limits. She glanced around the modern kitchen, probably still a part of the original house but updated considerably. Two doors led from the kitchen—one to the cellar and one to the rest of the house. If she wasn't afraid it would hurt Paul, she might have been tempted to take a peek—but no. The lighthouse was what drew her. The lighthouse held the secrets, she was sure of it. A beacon of light and hope. What other symbol would hold The Inheritance?

She silently saluted the still-sleeping beacon through the window. "We're close, Pop."

The father/daughter dance continued the celebration. Dessert appetizers had been laid out, and Paul shuffled across her line of sight, busy commanding his troops. The team cleaned up as pans of food emptied, and as each person finished his final chore, Paul sent him to the lighthouse. This was fair, but it also meant that Paul, Jessie, and Meranda had to wait.

Finally, as Meranda loaded the last of the dinner plates into the van, Paul touched her shoulder. "Let's go."

Jessie grinned behind him, and all three headed to the lighthouse. Meranda couldn't stop her feet from sprinting across the lawn.

Despite her excitement, she paused at the threshold, savoring every detail, allowing her senses to memorize the moment. The rough wooden door. The breeze as it whistled through the opening. In reverence she stepped through and into the small room built off the tower. Despite the cleanliness with not a cobweb in sight, there still lingered a musty smell. The smell of history. White walls inside the room mimicked the white stucco of the outside. The room couldn't have been bigger than a large camping tent and was very stark. No pictures. No curtains on the small leaded windows. But she didn't care. She walked where her great-great-grandfather had walked.

On the far side of the room, the entryway beckoned her. She stepped through and looked straight up. The cylinder was a geometric red-bricked marvel all the way up with a winding iron staircase creating visual art.

Paul and Jessie followed her up the steps as she ran her hands over the wall. "My great-great-grandfather touched every one of these bricks."

"Where do you suppose he would have hidden the coins?" Jessie's voice came from a few steps below.

Pulling herself from the awe of the moment, Meranda suddenly remembered why she was there. She glanced upward. "I don't know. Maybe up. The light draws people near. Perhaps it's a clue to draw us near the treasure."

They wound their way toward the top—Meranda, Paul, then Jessie. On the wall, small plaques had been mortared to the bricks. "Look! The pictures on these plaques are the same as on the coins."

"Pillars?"

"No, the other side. Where the crest is. See?" She pointed to one near his elbow. "A castle." Then one at her eye level. "A lion." She glanced up the tower and continued to climb. "They're staggered all the way up."

"No, Jessie." Paul admonished his assistant for something.

Meranda looked down through the waffle pattern of the metal steps but could only see a portion of Jessie's miffed expression.

"Well," her voice held an obstinate tone, "how will we know if we don't remove them?"

Meranda smiled at her enthusiasm. She had apparently tried to pry a plaque off the wall. Surely there must be a better option than demolishing the place.

Finally, the stairs reached a platform with a five-rung ladder leading through a square hole. Meranda began climbing, but her foot slipped on the second rung. She tumbled backward, and Paul caught her at the waist. His sudden, unexpected touch created the sensation of skittering minnows inside her stomach. She turned to look at his concerned face.

"You okay?"

"I'm fine, just a klutz." She continued to climb, torn between staying in the cradle of the gentle palms or continuing her quest. As her head cleared the hole, she encountered sneakered feet curtained by yellow gossamer silk. A feminine hand reached out and helped steady her as she climbed through the hole.

"Step to the side, please," the young woman said. Then she helped Paul and finally Jessie until they all stood on the platform with her, inches from the large lantern in the middle. Meranda reached out to touch it reverently. The heart of the lighthouse that symbolized family, heritage. . . Pop. Her chin trembled, but she willed it into submission.

"Please don't touch the light. I don't know why, but that's what I'm supposed to say." The woman offered an infectious smile. "My name is Glenys Bernard, sister and maid of honor to the bride." She curtsied, flouncing her frilly dress. The yellow did nothing for her coloring. Meranda could relate. They both had a red tinge to their hair, Glenys's lighter than Meranda's, but their skin tone was the same. *Blast.* She never would have had these thoughts if it weren't for her sister and mother.

They all introduced themselves. Meranda thought of sticking with her incognito name, Judith Francis, a blend of the first boat her ancestor commandeered and his name, but decided to honor Paul by using the honest approach. Thankfully, Glenys didn't seem to care that she had a dreaded Drake in her lighthouse.

"Nice shoes." Jessie pointed down at Glenys's feet.

"My dad asked me to play tour guide out here, so I kicked off the gold sandals and threw on the tennis shoes. These stairs are murder on heels." She cleared her throat, thrust her arm toward the light casing, and began to lecture. "This light is not the original light. That one resides in the Crossroads Bay Museum. A keeper who stayed in the house ran it. When automated lighthouses became popular, this light was installed. It has a sensor and turns on at dusk and off at dawn."

Jessie interrupted. "Do you know what the plaques represent?"

"Plaques?"

Jessie motioned down through the hole in the platform.

"Oh. The little pictures. I have no idea. They've always been there. My dad might know, though."

Meranda fingered her pendant from the chain. Should she share with this personable woman? Something about Glenys drew her in. Perhaps she could get to the judge through his daughter.

"I have this pendant that shows an image of the pillars on some of the plaques."

Glenys reached out and inspected the pendant. With wide eyes, she said, "This one looks like ours."

Meranda's neck tingled. "Two pendants?"

"Apparently, but ours has the image of the crest with the castles and the lions." She looked at the back. "And instead of this inscription, ours says IR1.345."

Meranda bounced on her toes, her excitement over this discovery about to ping her off the walls. Two pendants! That must mean something, but what? "How did you get it?"

"Believe it or not, it was hidden behind a brick in the kitchen, above the cellar door. When the kitchen was renovated a few years ago, the workers noticed the loose brick. Dad had the pendant appraised, but all they could tell us was that it was handmade. We keep it in a tin box on a shelf next to the cellar door."

"May I see it?"

"Sure, let's go back to the house." She motioned for them all to head back down the stairs.

On the way to the house, Jessie whispered to Meranda, "Do you think both pendants together would be considered valuable?"

"To me they would be, but if we found out they had been with the original coins, I wouldn't doubt some museum in England would pay a lot for Sir Francis Drake's property."

When they reached the house, Meranda hoped the judge would be distracted and not see her closely. But Glenys spotted him on the patio and asked him to join them in the kitchen when he got a chance.

They walked into the back of the house and into the kitchen, Meranda adjusting the wig to be sure she was still disguised. Glenys went to the cellar door and reached for a small box that sat with other knickknacks on a shelf to the left of the door. The lid had a tin top that showed a lighthouse in punch art. Meranda wondered how old the box was.

Glenys drew out a pendant with a leather cord and handed it to Meranda. "See? It's the same shape and style, but has a crest of lions and castles."

"This is the other side of the coins." Excitement surged through Meranda.

"Coins?" Glenys reached for the pendant and put it back in the box.

Meranda told her all she knew about The Inheritance.

"And you think they might be here somewhere?"

Meranda nodded. "More than likely in the lighthouse."

"Awesome!" Glenys's eyes sparkled like a child's on Christmas morning. "Oh, Daddy. . ."

Judge Bernard entered the room.

Meranda sidled behind Paul, using him as a shield. He shot a concerned glance over his shoulder, letting her know he understood her reticence.

Glenys hopped on her toes. "Daddy, I've just heard the coolest thing about the history of this place. But first, do you know anything about the plaques on the lighthouse walls?"

"I don't know." He scratched his nose. "A lot about this place is a mystery. The previous owner only bought it for an investment and didn't care about the history."

"And what about you?" Meranda clapped her hand over her loose lips, but too late. Her quick temper had just sunk her own ship, and now the judge glowered at her.

nine

"Excuse me?"

Meranda cleared her throat under his scrutiny. "I mean, the public hasn't been allowed in here for a long time. Don't you think it would be good for the community to be able to tour such an important artifact?"

"Oh, and Daddy, Meranda has a pendant just like ours." Glenys, oblivious to the tension that had just entered the room like a hungry shark, had unknowingly sliced and diced Meranda into a hearty meal for the judge.

He squinted at her. "You're that Drake woman." Meranda stood tall and removed the wig. But even through her bravado, her stomach held a tempest of emotion as she felt her dream capsizing.

The judge pointed at her. "Stay right there." He looked at Paul. "You, too." Jessie had disappeared. He stepped out a moment, leaving Meranda wondering what was in store for her. When he returned, he snapped at her. "I just called the police. I'm having you arrested for trespassing."

Paul stepped in front of her and confronted the judge. "Please, sir. Let me take the blame. She's part of my staff."

"Then I'll have you both hauled off."

Before long, Meranda and Paul were leaving in the backseat of a squad car, blinking their surprise at each other.

Paul stared out the window. Past him Meranda could see Jessie and the crew piling into the vans so they could follow them out.

Meranda wanted to read his face, but he continued to look out the window, even though it was now too dark to see anything. "I'm so sorry, Paul."

He turned pained eyes to her. "If my grandmother hears of this, all my hard work will be ruined."

She couldn't say it enough. "I'm sorry—"

"No." His voice still held venom. "I'm sorry for allowing you to do something that I knew was wrong. I compromised my integrity."

After a long silence, she spoke again, "You can't imagine how good it felt to finally stand in that lighthouse, to touch my family's history."

He shifted to further shut her out. "I'm happy for you then."

"I know I shouldn't have involved you, but I was blinded by the importance."

"And what is the importance?" He whipped his head around and glared at her. "Why are these coins worth losing your father's life and my career?"

"Because. . .I think my family is in financial trouble."

&

Her family needs the money? By the looks of her mother's house, that surprised Paul.

"How do you know?"

"Things are missing from the house. Artwork, antiques, jewelry, all gone with no explanation. Some of it was Pop's. It would stand to reason she'd get rid of his things. But the others. . ."

Her downturned mouth implied more to the story. Arguing in the home. Parents divorced. Daughters put in the middle.

"She loved my dad once."

Okay, Meranda needed to talk, and he was a captive listener. Might as well make the best of the situation. "Tell me about your dad."

The corners of her mouth curved upward into a tiny grin. "Believe it or not, Pop was a solid businessman. After he met my mom, her father, who was president at Crossroads Bank, offered him a job. Pop worked his way up to commercial loans and became the vice president."

"Hey, he probably helped my grandfather update the kitchen at our restaurant."

"I'm sure." She regarded her shoes. "He did very well. Moved us into the home you saw. But then the treasure called to him. He'd always been fascinated with the story of the coins and had contacted the maritime museum just for fun." Her grin turned into a full-blown smile. "He and I would go sailing, and he'd regale me with stories of the coins and the pirates that wanted them. All made up, of course. Pop was a dreamer."

"Sounds like he should have been a writer instead of a loan officer."

She tilted her head. "Interesting that you should say that. After he quit his job at the bank, he wrote down all of his pirate stories. He never did anything with them, but I've saved every one in notebooks."

"Why would he quit such a lucrative job?"

"So he could sail full-time. That's when he bought the charter boat."

"And that's when he left your mom?"

"Well, that's when she kicked him out."

It was becoming clearer now. The dreamer married the socialite who expected him to maintain her lifestyle.

"So, how did your dad get so caught up in the coins?"

Paul suddenly realized they had an audience. The patrolman in the front had become quiet. "We are allowed to talk to each other, right?"

He looked at them in the rearview mirror. "Please, go ahead. This is more entertaining than my dispatch radio."

Meranda frowned but continued. "Pop had known about the coins as a child, but it wasn't until the earthquake a decade ago that he became obsessed. The shipwreck was unearthed then. He knew the history behind the shipwreck and that Augustus built the lighthouse, but beyond that we just speculated. We contacted the Hawaiian Historical Society and learned through a journal that the last person known to have had the coins was Augustus's father, who had died before Augustus sailed to the mainland. So, it stood to reason that Augustus's older brother would have the coins. However, according to the museum records of Augustus's family tree, we knew his brother had died. We assumed Augustus ended up with the coins somehow, but it wasn't until I received the letter from the maritime museum that confirmed they had indeed been passed to him."

"Wow. You've done a lot of research to get to this point, haven't you?"

She nodded, suddenly looking very weary even while talking about her passion. "So, if the coins aren't in the lighthouse, does that take you back to the shipwreck?"

"I don't know." She closed her eyes.

They pulled into the station parking lot and were ushered inside. A deputy met them and informed the officer who had brought them in to take off their handcuffs. To Paul and Meranda he said, "You're both free to go."

Paul's heart stopped. Had his grandmother found out and put up bail? Would that even happen so soon? He knew nothing about being arrested.

The young deputy pulled them aside. "I'm sorry, folks. Seems Judge Bernard just wanted to put a scare into you."

Meranda's eyes flashed hot. "False arrest? Can he do that?"

He raised his palm. "According to the judge, he had told you to stay off his property. He was well within his rights to remove you. But he just called to drop the charges and said he hoped the squad car ride had been enough to let you know he was serious." He rubbed the back of his neck. "And frankly, I'm okay with it because it means less paperwork."

"I can't believe this! Seriously?" Meranda stomped her foot and looked ready to punch someone.

"Don't argue with the man," Paul whispered. "We're about to be set free."

She continued to fume as he steered her to a set of black plastic chairs along a far wall. He pulled out his cell phone and called Jessie, asking her to come pick them up. Jessie promised to be there in ten minutes.

When they walked out of the building and stepped into the night air, Paul took a deep breath.

Freedom. And Abuelita was none the wiser.

ten

"Pablo, what is this?"

Abuelita waved the morning newspaper under his nose as he chopped onions in the restaurant kitchen. The heading of an article about the lighthouse wedding caused his eyes to sting—or was that the sudden pungency of his onion-saturated hands? He stabbed the knife into the cutting board, snatched the paper out of her fingers, and began reading.

> ## BERNARD WEDDING MARRED BY CRASHER
> *Despite Judge Gordon Bernard's attempt to hold a private wedding, a party crasher still managed to get through his defenses. Soon after his daughter Alison Theresa Bernard said 'I do' to Daniel Domingo Lopez this last Saturday, the judge discovered an uninvited guest. Meranda Drake, who owns a charter boat business out of the Crossroads Bay marina, had smuggled herself into the wedding using Tapas Mediterranean Delights Catering where she posed as an employee. Paul Godfrey, the owner of the catering company, admitted to helping the woman. He was also arrested, but charges for both people were later dropped.*

Paul set the paper down, squeezed his eyes shut, and swallowed the dread creeping up his throat. When he opened them again, Abuelita stood there with her arms folded. "You did not tell me."

He grabbed the knife and began mincing the onion into tinier pieces than he had intended as he took his frustration out on the unsuspecting root. "It's no big deal. Meranda wanted to see the lighthouse, and she was willing to work for us to do that." He hoped his excuse didn't sound as lame as he knew it to be.

"The company's name is mentioned." She grabbed the paper and shook it in her tiny fist.

"But the article clears us."

"It is bad publicity." She smacked the paper against her hand. "People will remember that you were blamed. They won't remember that the charges were dropped." She pushed her lower lip into her upper. Paul felt a grin tug at his cheek despite the scolding and tried to remain respectful, even though Abuelita looked like a miniature bulldog.

"Who is Meranda?"

Paul cocked his head back and let out a groan. He didn't want to have to explain Meranda when he didn't understand her himself. "You remember. She's the one who recommended us for her sister's wedding. The Drakes?"

A smile played on her face, and he knew she was counting the dollar signs that account would pull in. "Ah. They ordered lots of food."

"Right. Lots of food, tons of it."

Her eyes suddenly twinkled. "Oh! Pablo, I get it." She walked out of the kitchen and into the empty dining room.

Paul followed. He should leave this one alone. Abuelita was happy, even though he had no idea why. "What? What do you get?"

"You have feelings for her, sí?" She waved her twiglike finger and chortled. "Your abuelo and I started out much the same."

"No, it's not like that. . . ." Well, okay, it was. But that's not why Meranda was at the lighthouse. Then again, maybe it was better Abuelita thought that.

She pivoted and faced him. "Oh. She has not returned your heart."

"No—I mean—"

"I will work on that." With a curt nod, she headed toward the front door and unlocked it for the lunch crowd.

Paul stood in the middle of the dining room, horror replacing the dread he'd felt earlier. Abuelita would stop at nothing to play matchmaker.

☙

Meranda arrived at her boat on Tuesday morning dressed in old jeans and a T-shirt. She had no charters that day, so she decided to do some painting on the *Golden Hind*. Her police scare three days prior had put her in the mood to make things new.

She thought about Paul, how he lived by honesty. Yet whenever she tried it, she got no reward. Only grief. Paul was a Christian, but so what?

When Pop died, God didn't care about her or her family. He took away a good man, leaving his loved ones to fend for themselves.

Her mind continued to ramble as she went back to the parking lot for supplies. It took her a couple of trips to lug paint, pans, brushes, and tarps to the boat from her truck. On the final trip, she happened to glance toward the *Romanda Jule*.

What? She dropped the paint trays with a clatter. Running to the slip—the empty slip—she looked around frantically for the boat. Had she not tied it after taking Paul out the other day? No, she remembered showing him how they did it.

No doubt about it. Someone had stolen her boat. Her stomach churned. How could she lose one more representation of Pop?

She pulled out her cell phone and called the coast guard. After stammering through the explanation, a bored voice told her someone would be arriving to file a report.

Her legs suddenly felt like limp seaweed. She lowered herself to the dock, sitting cross-legged with her head in her hands.

I'm sorry, Pop. I can't seem to do anything right. I've abandoned Mom to the point where she won't confide in me. I've lied for the sake of the coins. I've been hauled to jail. She wiped the tears off her cheeks. *I need you.*

Her cell phone rang. It was a woman from the sheriff's department.

"Miss Drake, I did a check on your boat, and it seems to have been repossessed."

Meranda's stomach no longer merely churned. It felt like an entire sea gale was crashing inside. "Excuse me? How can that be possible? My father bought this boat for my sisters and me." She had no idea there were still payments on it.

"I'm sorry." The woman's steady voice calmed her somewhat. "I suggest you contact your bank if you feel there's been an error. Is there anything else I can do for you?"

Meranda thought of Paul. What would he do? "Pray." She snorted the word, not really meaning to.

"I can certainly do that for you, as soon as we hang up."

A few minutes later Meranda held her phone and stared at it. Would that woman really pray for her? Sure sounded like she would.

Suddenly buoyed by the kindness of this stranger, she called the bank and made an appointment with the loan officer for later that morning.

After stowing away her paint and supplies, she went back home to change. On the way, she called Rose and apprised her of the situation.

"Oh, Mer, I'm so sorry."

"I wonder if Mom is paying any bills at all. Is anything else missing that she could have sold?"

"Not that I've found, but perhaps the bill paying would be next. You look into this, and I'll investigate here at home."

"Thanks, Ro. I'm glad we have each other."

"Always."

At home Meranda threw on a short-sleeved tailored shirt and tan slacks. May had arrived and with it warmer temperatures.

Once she walked into the bank, she knew exactly where to go. She passed the picture of her grandfather Muldoon, his stern eyes so like her mother's. Patrick Cooper stood and greeted her as she entered his office. She hadn't seen him in more than a year, and his dark hair seemed more speckled with gray.

"How are you doing, Meranda?" His honest blue eyes crinkled at the corners. She always liked Pat and his humble attitude.

"I'm not doing so well, Pat. My boat is gone."

"Well, let's see what happened." He started clicking keys on his computer. "Thirteen months ago there were several missed payments."

"Right after Pop died."

"Yes." The small word held a ton of compassion. "Looks like we sent out reminders, set up a partial payment plan. . ." He continued to search the screen. "Those were only sent for three months, then they stopped." He leaned back in his chair. "There were only six months of payments left."

She swallowed hard as she worked the math in her head.

"Meranda." He folded his hands on his desk. "I knew your father and respected him while he worked here. I wouldn't tell just any customer this, but I think you deserve to know."

Was that a disclaimer on his lips?

"He didn't manage his money very well. He took out several loans to fund his diving expeditions."

"How could he have worked at this bank and not managed his own money?"

"It happens more often than you realize. I fear that he overextended."

"Is that why my mother is selling her valuables? What happened to the insurance money?"

"It's possible that all went to pay for the expeditions, which would leave your family with only your incomes to stay afloat."

"My mother doesn't work outside the home. And Julianne still has student loans. Rose doesn't have a job, either." Meranda closed her eyes. She seemed to be the only one of the four with a career. "It's up to me to keep the house from meeting the same fate as my boat."

"Or"—Pat raised his brows, reminding her of Pop when he reprimanded his girls—"you could tell your mother and sisters that if they want to keep their home, they're going to have to get their own jobs. It won't hurt them to be responsible." Only Pat could get away with this kind of talk. "I'm sure your business does very well, but I doubt it's enough to support your family to the point of keeping them in their house."

She drew in a big breath. He was right. She couldn't shoulder this responsibility alone. But one thing she could do. "I want my boat back. How much is owed?"

Meranda paid the rest of the balance, which made a dent in her savings account, but once the title was switched over, the boat would be solely hers. Pat told her where to pick it up.

More than ever she needed to find those coins. Even though they had been in the family for generations, when it came to her own little family unit, she would sell the coins in a heartbeat to protect those she loved.

As she drove away from the bank, she realized how much she needed Paul's paella and perhaps his gentle smile. When she arrived at Tapas, the place buzzed with activity as patrons flocked for the noon meal.

An elderly Spanish woman greeted her. "How many?"

Meranda held up one finger. "Just me, unless Paul is here and can join me."

"He is here." The woman puckered her face. "But he is much too busy to take his lunch."

Meranda consulted her watch. She was starving, but despite

her craving, she realized she was there to see Paul. "Perhaps I should come back another time."

A slow smile eased onto the old woman's face. "Ah. You are Meranda."

"Yes, I am." Heat flushed Meranda's cheeks. Had Paul been talking about her? Whatever could he have said?

"Oh, come with me then." The woman clapped her hands in two short bursts, and someone else took her place. "I have just the table for you."

She led her to a cozy alcove in the back where the lighting was dim. "Allow me." A match appeared in her hand, and a flame ignited from a candle resting in a red globe. "Ah, sí. I will go get Pablo."

How odd. A moment ago she had pictured Paul chained to the stove. Now this octogenarian, obviously his grandmother, seemed capable of freeing him.

He burst through a swinging door as if pushed, a bewildered look on his face. The sleeves of his white tailored shirt were rolled to his forearms, revealing brown skin. Then he saw her. His shy grin and the way he slipped his hands into his pockets made him look like a teenager on his first date.

Meranda felt a pleasant sensation in her stomach, and it wasn't from the anticipation of food. She felt like his prom date, for goodness' sake.

He slipped into the horseshoe-shaped booth but kept a respectable distance between them.

"Hi."

"Hi."

Scintillating conversation. But the way the candlelight warmed his mahogany-colored eyes—eyes that gazed at her appreciatively—it didn't matter if they used one-word sentences for a half hour. She realized at that moment that she liked this man. Really liked him.

"So, you came to eat by candlelight?" Both eyebrows rose as

he swept his hand toward the globe.

"Not my idea." Meranda began playing with a curl that tickled the side of her face. "You have a very forceful hostess. She insisted I sit here."

His gaze traveled up and over the walls that cupped the table. "That was my grandmother. This is where she seats special guests."

"Am I special?"

"I believe you are."

Meranda grabbed her cloth napkin and started fanning herself.

"So, what can I do for you?" His lips curved in a pleasant smile.

"Um. . ." A waitress brought glasses of water, and Meranda gulped down a quarter of hers. Why was she acting this way? The candlelight? The romantic Spanish music—wasn't it fiesta-style when she first walked in? The gorgeous man across from her who could cook—which was every woman's dream? "Food!"

He arched his brow.

"I mean, of course, I'm here for food. But I don't have a menu."

The corners of his eyes crinkled. "Let me choose for you. It will only take a few minutes, and I'll prepare it with my own hands."

Yep. She was feeling better already.

He slipped back into the kitchen, and she leaned her cheek on her hand as the morning's disappointment ebbed away. She needed this oasis in the midst of her crazy life.

Her cell phone chirped with a text message. Rose managed to get across her angst with only the letters on her phone. *MOM IS DRIVING ME CRAZY!*

Blast. Rose had impeccable timing. Meranda replied with, *I'LL CALL YOU LATER. CAN'T TALK NOW.* When Rose learned

Meranda was about to have lunch with the attractive chef, the one she'd already picked out for Meranda, she'd understand.

Soon enough Paul returned, both arms laden with plates. It was one thing for a guy to cook for you, but quite another for him to serve you. Meranda fanned herself again.

She motioned toward the kitchen. "Who's minding the restaurant?"

"Albert. And my grandmother."

"She gets around, doesn't she?"

He grabbed his napkin and flicked it like a whip. "You have no idea."

Before they began eating, he reached for her hand. Her heart leaped in her chest, causing happy ripples. But he said, "Do you mind if we pray?"

Pray? She would have pulled back if his touch hadn't sent such enjoyable tingles up her arm. Now she didn't know how she should feel.

❧

". . .bless this food to nourish our bodies. In Jesus' name, amen." Paul looked up from the prayer, still not believing that this woman was in his restaurant and apparently enjoying his company. But she pulled her hand away quickly and avoided his eyes. Had he been too forward? With the commanding Captain Meranda Drake? Surely not.

To cover the awkward silence, Paul asked if she had her necklace with her. She removed it from her neck, and he flipped it over in his fingers, inspecting the engraving on the back. "JG.IG. Two initials?"

"That's what I thought at first, but Judge Bernard's pendant is different."

Paul pulled a small spiral notebook from his breast pocket and consulted it. "IR1.345. They can't be dates."

"Unless they're encrypted. But why? If you're going to create an artifact, why not put the date on there for generations later to know exactly when it was made?"

"And they can't be initials like you had thought because of the three-digit number on the judge's pendant." She rested her elbow on the table and placed her chin on her fist. "Unless mine holds the initials and his holds the date. But still, his doesn't look like a date."

Paul rubbed his thumb over the letters. "These weren't etched by a professional."

He handed the pendant back to her. "When Glenys revealed she had a second pendant, you seemed excited to hear that news. I would think you'd be disappointed you didn't have the only one of its kind."

She placed her elbow on the table and leaned forward. "Think about it. Two pendants. That tells me my shipwrecked ancestor had one that he wore and kept the other near the coins. Of course, that's just a guess."

"Ah." Paul nodded. "So two pendants was another clue."

"Exactly."

"What makes you think they're in the lighthouse and not in the judge's home?"

"Because the plaques are in the lighthouse."

"But what about the pendant behind the brick in the kitchen of the main house?"

"Good point. Either could be right."

"I've been praying that you'll get your answers soon."

She pursed her lips and began stabbing the chicken on her plate. Not to pick it up, but to torture it.

"That is okay, isn't it?" Hope suddenly fled out the door that this woman would at least be open to the gospel.

"Do what you want, but I'm wondering why God would care."

He reached out to touch her forearm. "God cares."

Paul vowed to lead her on the faith journey just as Ruthanne, his alpaca-loving friend, had done for him.

eleven

Paul pushed his plate away knowing the food would settle like rocks in his stomach. "Why would you think God wouldn't care?"

"He didn't do much for my dad, did He?" Vehemence sparked from her words.

Paul winced as if the verbal blow had been meant for him personally. "I'm sorry about your father." What could he say to this hurting soul? He prayed for wisdom. "I've lost people close to me, too. After my mom died, anger wanted to eat me up from the inside out. And it probably would have if I hadn't trusted that God knew what He was doing."

He gauged whether he should go on, not wanting to push her further away from God. Even though she remained silent, he sensed the Lord pressing him to continue. "May I share a verse from the Bible that has held me together in my darkest times?" She tipped her head, and he went on. " 'I have been crucified with Christ and I no longer live, but Christ lives in me. The life I live in the body, I live by faith in the Son of God, who loved me and gave himself for me.' This verse from Galatians 2:20 tells me that no matter what my eyes see, I trust that God has my best interests at heart."

"It's a choice for you, then."

"Yes. Because I'm still in this old, sinful body." He pinched the skin on his shoulders. "I can so easily get caught up in the what-ifs of life. What if I could have made my mother's last days better for her? What if I hadn't run out on my grandmother to live with my aunt and uncle? What if I hadn't run back home after someone I thought I loved fell for someone else?" He smiled and reached for her hand again. "About that last one, perhaps it was God's will so we could meet." And so he could share his faith with her.

The brooding frown on her brow released its hold, and a small grin played on her face. "Perhaps you should hold that thought until you've gotten to know me better."

"Perhaps I won't be disappointed."

Continuing to hold onto his hand as if it were a lifeline, she closed her eyes and leaned her temple onto the knuckles of her other hand. He didn't know if she was praying or just trying to gain control.

Her cell phone rang. *Arrgh. . .Arrgh. . .* A happy pirate tone that contrasted with their conversation. "That's probably my sister." She released his hand—dare he think reluctantly?—and frowned at the ID. "No, maybe it's a charter client."

She answered, and her eyes registered surprise. "Oh hi, Glenys. . . What? Certainly you don't think I took it." Meranda wrapped her hand around the mouthpiece and whispered to Paul. "The other pendant is gone."

Paul's stomach dipped, but then he realized they couldn't blame them since they had an alibi involving handcuffs and a patrol car.

Meranda relaxed as she spoke to Glenys. Apparently she'd only called to inform her of the theft.

After Meranda hung up, she said, "Glenys wants to help look for the coins. She suggested meeting at the museum at two o'clock to inspect the original lighthouse lamp. Her dad is still angry with me, though, and would rather I stay away from the lighthouse."

"Does he understand that we couldn't have taken the other pendant?"

"Yes. There were still people milling about, but Glenys said she can't imagine any of them would have wanted it. There will be an investigation, but we're in the clear. As far as visiting the lighthouse again, she said she's working on him. I think I've made a friend."

"She seems like a good person and is probably sorry you got into so much trouble."

"Us." She pointed between her and him.

"True."

"I'd love to tag along to the museum if you don't mind. I don't have a catering job, and things are dead around here about that time of day."

Her slow smile made his heart beat faster. "I'd like to go to the library after lunch, but I'll come back here afterward to pick you up."

He could have sat there with her forever, but knew the little Spanish cupid in the kitchen would come after him if they became swamped. He stood and headed for the kitchen but turned back before pushing the kitchen door. "Two o'clock."

"I'll be here."

In the kitchen, Abuelita stood at the range, stirring the stew. "How did it go, Pablo?"

He grabbed his apron from the hook on the wall and tied the strings in back. "How did what go?" He knew what she was asking. Seriously. Candlelight? Soft music? The *love* alcove?

"Miss Drake. She return your affection now, sí?"

He kissed his abuelita's wiry hair. "It's in God's hands."

"Then I pray." With a satisfied smile on her face, she handed him the spoon and trotted out to the dining room.

He would pray also, that Meranda would soon choose the right path toward God.

❧

Meranda finished her lunch and headed to the library just around the block. She decided to walk since the day had turned out beautiful. Spring azaleas and rhododendrons provided color in large cement pots along the sidewalk provided by the town.

While walking, she called her sister back. "What's up, sis?"

"Your mother has gone over the top." Rose's voice held all the frustration that Meranda felt.

"*My* mother? Have you disowned her now?" *Join the club.*

"She's taken over the wedding. Things have gotten out of control."

Meranda gripped the phone. "Is she continuing to pour money into this?"

"Yes. I no longer have a soloist. I have a choral ensemble." Disgust colored her sister's voice.

Would it be too much to ask that she'd found a volunteer group from her social status church? "What is she paying them?"

"She won't tell me, but it's a group one of her friends recommended. They tour the nation and just happened to be in town at that time."

Big bucks. "Rose, you've got to curtail her spending. She can't afford it."

"I know. But how can I stop her? She doesn't listen to a thing I say." A slight pause. "What am I going to do?"

Get a backbone and say no hovered on her lips, but she decided to temper her words. "Listen, only you can stop this madness. Be firm with her. You never wanted your wedding to be the event of the season."

"No, and it doesn't help that Mrs. St. James is helping to fuel the fire. My future mother-in-law seems to think that just because our name is on several businesses in town that we are higher on the social scale."

"Yeah, thanks to the founding Drake, Mom has had her head in the clouds for too long." She walked through the library, perusing the reference section. "What does Steven think of all this?"

"He's so clueless. 'Whatever you want, Mother.' I don't think he can stand up to his mom any more than I can to mine."

"Stay strong, Ro. This isn't her wedding, it's yours."

"Thanks. I just need to hear that once in a while."

Meranda hung up, furious with her mother. Would this be one of those times to *choose* to trust God? It made more sense to believe if man messes something up, man must fix it. But there was no fixing her mother. She was a barge with a full hull of ideas that didn't make a lick of sense to anyone else. There was no stopping her.

She decided to put God to the test. *Paul says I must choose to trust You.* She thrust her gaze heavenward. *How about it, God? Can You stop her from destroying herself and dragging us along with her?*

While she killed time at the library, she read about lighthouses and their various types of lamps. She didn't hold much hope that the coins would be in the old Crossroads Bay lantern. But, since Glenys suggested it, perhaps there would be more hope of Meranda visiting the lighthouse in the future.

Just before two o'clock, she dumped four books into her truck and headed back to the restaurant.

Paul's grandmother was now bussing tables. Was there nothing this woman couldn't do? By the looks of the dining room, they'd had quite a midday crowd.

"Abuelita." Paul walked out of the kitchen rolling down his shirtsleeves. "You don't have to do that."

When he spotted Meranda and smiled, warmth cascaded over her like the sun coming out on a drizzly day.

"I must keep busy, sí?" The mini senior citizen continued loading a square plastic container with dirty dishes and silverware. Fortunately it was sitting on a rolling cart, so she didn't have to lug it back to the kitchen.

He kissed her on top of her head. "I'll be back in time for the dinner rush."

She placed a tiny fist on her hip. With the corners of her lips drawn down and a scowl on her face, she asked, "Where are you going?"

He motioned toward Meranda. His grandmother shaded her eyes and peered at her. "Oh! Meranda? Come here, you are standing with the sun glaring behind you. I did not see you."

Meranda moved into the dining room. Only four tables were occupied now. With a firm grip, the woman grabbed Meranda's upper arm and peered up at her with snapping gray brown eyes. "What do you think of my Pablo?"

"Abuelita!" Paul's face went crimson. Even though Meranda was just as embarrassed by the question, his shocked look entertained her.

She patted the elderly hand on her arm. "I think he must be a wonderful grandson, and he obviously loves you very much."

The older woman looked at Paul. "I like her."

Paul finally recovered and gently freed Meranda from his grandmother's grip. "I'm glad she has your stamp of approval." He glanced at Meranda. "You two haven't been properly introduced. Meranda Drake, this is my abuelita, my grandmother, Carmen Espinoza."

She held out her hand and received a warm, but firm, handshake.

"You may call me Abuelita."

ॐ

As they walked out a moment later, Paul shook his head. "Wow. I've never seen that happen before." He looked back at the door, befuddled at his ever-changing abuelita.

"What?"

"She has never told someone she's just met to address her so informally."

"Then I'm flattered."

"You should be, and maybe a little frightened. The next time you come to eat, she may put you to work."

Meranda laughed. "That would be fine with me."

That would be fine with him, too.

They decided to go in one car, his, and they drove across town to the museum. When they got there, Glenys was waiting outside the brick building.

Meranda marched in, leading the other two. "I've been here countless times with my father." As if to demonstrate, she nodded at a fortyish security guard sitting behind a counter. "Hi, Norm."

He saluted two-finger style from his eyebrow.

They entered the room that housed the light, along with other local artifacts, and gathered around the heavy lamp displayed on the floor. Paul felt dwarfed next to it. The polished brass and crystal lenses made this a true testament to man's achievements.

Glenys took her tour-guide stance and motioned toward the monstrosity. "This lamp used a five-wick kerosene burner and a fixed Fresnel lens, meaning it didn't move. Note the narrow panes of glass, creating the prism look."

Brass piping separated the panes of glass, and the whole assembly resembled a huge Christmas ornament. Paul remembered seeing something similar in a miniversion on Abuelita's tree every year.

Glenys continued. "The panes redirected the light so it could be seen farther, squeezing it, if you will, into beams that pierced the darkness. It was later converted to electricity with a rotating lens, the one that's in the lighthouse now. A few years after that it went automatic, so a keeper was no longer needed."

Meranda gazed at Glenys. "I'm beginning to think you love the lighthouse as much as I do."

"When my dad bought it, I was eleven. I always loved coming here in the summers and playing." She regarded Meranda with a serious face. "I'm here often to retreat from my crazy life in Hollywood. My mom grounded us in good old-fashioned Christian values. I feel God's presence at the lighthouse every time I see the ocean crash over the rocks or watch a storm come in."

Now Paul definitely approved of this friendship. He watched Meranda carefully for her reaction, but her face held no animosity.

"As far as I'm concerned," Glenys continued, "you can visit me anytime."

Meranda pulled her into a hug. "Thank you."

Paul felt a glow in his heart as he watched this friendship form. He began pacing around the lamp. Meranda took over the tour guide role and led them to a wall, pointing to a print of a painted portrait. "This is Augustus Drake."

Paul noted the family resemblance despite the trim white beard on the mature face. Piercing eyes, gray, and full of adventure. This man knew how to live.

Meranda moved to another print, this one of a white ship with four masts. Multiple sails billowed from each mast. "This is the *Victoria Jane,* the ship that now lies off our coast. This clipper belonged to a fleet of sugar ships built for the sugar trade in Hawaii. Augustus had decided to travel to Hawaii to be with his family when his brother died." She moved down the wall to show them a series of printed out facts under artist renderings of the ship in the storm.

"On the way back," Meranda summed up, "the ship encountered a storm and began taking on water. They tried to limp back here, but she didn't have it in her. After the shipwreck, Augustus and a few of the crew made it to shore. He decided to build the lighthouse in memory of the lives that were lost." That was the end of the facts, but Meranda continued. "Augustus never sold it, but when he died, the family must have decided not to keep it."

"That's why the coins have to be there." Paul drew his gaze from the articles and back to the lamp. "Or here." He paced around the lamp again, peering at it as though it were a huge diamond needing an appraisal.

Meranda joined him as he circled. "The only relatives Augustus had here were a wife and a teenage boy. His sister lived in San Francisco. I don't have any documentation of her trying to find the coins after Augustus's death." She stopped circling and frowned. "I don't think there's room for coins here." Disappointment colored her tone, but she continued to prowl around the object.

"The Drake family sold the property in the 1940s," Glenys continued the lineage.

"To the one who put the gate up," Meranda spoke with vehemence as she continued to pace the lamp.

Glenys nodded. "Instead of tearing it down, my dad mechanized it." She cast an apologetic glance to Meranda. "The guy we bought the property from sixteen years ago was never there. He just wanted it for an investment. We had a lot of fixing up to do, but my dad was determined to restore the two buildings as much as he could to their original states."

Meranda glanced up from her examination. "Tell your father thank you from me." Her gaze moved to Paul, who smiled his agreement. She grinned back, then went back to the lamp.

Glenys moved down the wall. "This is interesting." She stopped at a framed newspaper clipping.

"What have you got there? A clue?" Paul called to her.

"No," she answered while stroking the frame. "Just a picture of my property in a newspaper clipping from 1907."

He left Meranda at the lamp and joined Glenys.

The article heading under the picture stated, "AUGUSTUS

DRAKE OPENS ARMS TO FAMILIES." In the picture an older Drake stood with his arms outstretched at the end of the forked road—the lighthouse in the distance to the left and the house to the right. "The article says," Glenys spoke with an emotional thickness in her voice, "Augustus held his first benefit for the families who lost their loved ones in the shipwreck during the dedication. He sold tours into the lighthouse to raise money for them, then invited them onto his property and fed them." She glanced at Meranda. "Your ancestor was a great man."

Meranda left the lamp to stand between Paul and Glenys. Paul felt her hand slip through his arm and noticed she did the same with Glenys. Silently, they paid homage to a man with an open-door policy and a heart of gold.

twelve

For the next week Meranda kept busy with whale-watching excursions. The lighthouse continued to be her source of strength, a tall sentinel watching over her.

"We're close, Pop," she whispered as she stopped the boat in deep waters. While the fifteen passengers watched the western horizon for whale spouts, she turned in her seat topside and reached for her binoculars. She quickly found the lighthouse lamp in the lenses and followed the structure down to the twin pillars that marked the path to the beach. Odd that she hadn't noticed how they resembled the art on her pendant. But even now she had to strain to see them as they blended in with the white stucco of the lighthouse.

Now that she thought about it, the pillars were in an odd spot. Why not have the steps lead down from the house? The slope was gentler there. From where her boat sat in the water, the lighthouse was perfectly framed between the pillars. The back of her neck tingled. This had to be a clue.

Suddenly her mind's eye flickered to Paul. They had spoken on the phone nearly every day since their trip to the museum. She loved the way he had championed her in front of the judge when he called the police on her. Then the shy way he slipped his hands into his pockets when he saw her at the restaurant sitting in the alcove. Shyness and protectiveness. Two facets to this man whom she found herself eager to learn more about.

When she arrived home that evening, she called Paul's cell phone to invite him on the *Romanda Jule* for the next day, knowing it was his day off from the restaurant. She hoped he didn't have any catering jobs. She mostly wanted to get to know him, but also thought they could brainstorm the coins together while enjoying an outing.

"Do I get to drive?" His voice held a smile.

"Would that keep you from getting seasick?"

"Yes. It definitely would."

"I think you just pretend to get nauseous so you can drive my boat."

"You got me. My pasty white face? Makeup. The sweat on my upper lip? From a squirt bottle in my pocket."

"Okay! I get it." She laughed. "I think it's a control issue. Do you feel the same about airplanes?"

"Um. . .well. . ." He paused, and she took that as an admission, but then she heard him talking to someone in the background.

"I know you're still at work, so I'll let you go," Meranda said.

"No problem. I was just talking to Jessie. She overheard our conversation and wondered if she could come, too. And since we're brainstorming, what about Glenys?"

Okay, now her cozy twosome just turned into a foursome.

When she agreed, Paul said, "Great. Can you call Glenys?"

"Sure, I still have her number in my phone from when she called me."

The next morning, Glenys showed up first. Meranda waved to her from the *Romanda Jule* when she saw her standing at the dock entrance searching the boats and looking confused. Glenys smiled and waved back. With her hand still in the air, a seagull swooped her hand, apparently checking if she held a morsel he could steal. The young woman shrieked and ran in circles as if trying to escape a swarm of bees.

Meranda ran to her. She stopped the frenzy by grasping her shoulders. "Glenys, it's okay. It was just a seagull."

Glenys covered her hair with both hands, but slowly

lowered them as she seemed to focus on Meranda. "Yeah. Of course. Just a seagull."

Meranda escorted her to the boat, but Glenys continued to watch the sky with a wary eye. She relaxed once she settled herself into the boat and so did Meranda. One phobia at a time was all she could handle.

A few minutes later Paul arrived with Jessie and her boyfriend, Derrick, whom Meranda had only met the day she crashed the lighthouse wedding. But that was okay. With more people they would soon have a regular parley about the coins.

Paul still hesitated slightly as he stepped on deck.

"Still having qualms?" She placed her hand on his arm.

"Oh yeah, but at least I'm here of my own accord. Must be a breakthrough of some kind."

They went to the helm under the canopy as Derrick and Glenys made themselves comfortable on deck. Paul had brought snacks, and Jessie put them in the galley.

Meranda motioned for him to sit in the captain's chair. But before he did, he said, "I have a surprise for you." He reached into his back pocket and pulled out his wallet.

"Money?" She clapped her hands together in mock surprise.

"Better." He drew out a card and showed it to her.

"An Oregon Boater Education Card? How did you do this so fast?" Her heart raced when she realized she'd made a convert of a die-hard landlubber.

"Many nights on the Internet taking the course." He rubbed his eyes and fake yawned. "Made the day job a little risky, but I only lost one finger while dicing carrots." He held up his hand, back toward her, his ring finger crooked into his palm.

Ignoring his warped humor, she threw her arms wide and hugged him. "This is totally awesome!"

Meranda could have remained in the hug, but remembering

the others, pulled away from Paul and waved his card. "Ladies and gentleman, I present your captain for the day."

Jessie moaned. But her smile belied her words. "Someone notify my family. I may not be going home."

Paul sat, and Meranda oriented him again on the controls. When she felt confident he knew what he was doing, she gave the go-ahead to start the engine.

He began to pull away from the dock, and Meranda placed her hand on his arm. "Um, Paul. Did you remember to untie us from the dock?"

"No!"

"Relax. I did it. But that's something the captain should always check."

Paul's face turned the same color as her maid-of-honor dress, dark pink. It looked better on him than on her. "Got it. No dragging dock behind us."

They headed out to sea, and he opened the throttle until they were skimming along at a fine clip. Once they were near the place she'd seen whales the day before, she asked him to slow the boat to a stop.

"Like a pro." Meranda patted his back, pleased he'd conquered his fear.

"And now," he said as he cut the engine, "I'm hungry. I brought some cold appetizers. Interested?"

"Race you!" She led him down into the galley while the other guests enjoyed the sunshine on deck. As he scooted in next to her to reach the tiny refrigerator, he knocked a book to the floor that had been sitting on a small two-person table.

"I'm sorry. Man, what a klutz." He bent over to pick it up.

"No harm. Look inside."

He did, and his eyes grew wide as he perused the pages. "What is this?"

"One of Augustus Drake's journals. I brought it today to search for clues again."

"How long have you had this?" He continued to flip pages.

"About a year and a half. My dad found it through the San Francisco Maritime Museum. They have an exhibition dedicated to shipbuilding. This was in their storeroom because they already had a similar item on display."

"Wow. It details parts bought, cargo loaded, times the ships left and arrived back at port. Hey, look. Here's an entry from today's date, May 9, 1906." He read aloud. " 'Set out with beloved new bride to Hawaii. We passed over the grave of the *Victoria Jane* and said a prayer for those lost a year ago.' He also included scripture. ' "So when this corruptible shall have put on incorruption, and this mortal shall have put on immortality, then shall be brought to pass the saying that is written, Death is swallowed up in victory." 1 Cor. 15:54.' "

Meranda looked over his shoulder at the entry. "I don't know much more about my great-great-grandmother. I'm assuming he was taking her to meet his brother's family."

He skimmed a few more pages. "No mention of The Inheritance?"

She shook her head. "At this point, the lighthouse would have been nearly finished. I'm sure the coins were safe and sound."

They stood together for a moment in the small space, him reading, her watching him read. His intensity as he turned the pages assured her that he truly was interested in Augustus. Finally he handed the journal back.

He placed his hand on her arm and squeezed gently. "What a legacy you have, Meranda." His gaze locked on hers, and he drew her closer. Just as she stepped into what promised to be a warm embrace and a very pleasant first kiss, joyful pandemonium broke out on deck.

"Hey, you two!" Jessie called to them. "There are whales out here."

"Cool!" Glenys's voice. "Spouts. . .no! I see whole backs of whales! Get out here before you miss them."

"Don't they realize"—Paul's breath tickled her ear—"that you see whales nearly every day?"

"It's a whole pod!" Jessie again.

"I guess we'd better join them before they come looking for us." Meranda reluctantly stepped away and opened the drawer where she kept her bag. She tossed the journal inside, closed the drawer, then headed up the steps, Paul trailing with a sliced fruit tray for their midmorning snack.

Sure enough, there were about six young whales migrating south. Meranda stood at the railing enjoying them with the others, but what she enjoyed more was Paul standing behind her, his hand on her waist.

As the whales moved away, the five in the boat seated themselves in a loose ring. Jessie turned and said, "Hey, great driving earlier, boss. You didn't throw us overboard once."

"I learned from the best." He winked at Meranda, who maddeningly felt her cheeks warm like a teenager's.

"We decided my fear is a control issue."

Jessie laughed. "Your control issue must be something you got from your grandmother."

The morning passed quickly with no more whales, but Meranda enjoyed the others' company. She found she had a lot in common with Jessie, beyond the fact that their fathers knew each other.

At one point Jessie asked, "Do you dive, Meranda?"

"Yes. I used to dive with my father all the time."

"Have you ever gone crabbing off the jetty?" Jessie's eyes danced.

"I've done that a few times. I love chasing them and trying to stick them into bags." Meranda laughed.

"I like bringing them home and cooking them."

"I'll bet you cook up a mean Dungeness crab, don't you?"

Jessie tipped her head. "I'd like to think so."

"How do you cook them, Jess?" The topic turned to recipes when Paul got involved.

And this made Meranda hungry. She brought out the lunch fare Paul had brought.

While they enjoyed spicy marinated mushrooms, vegetable sticks and artichoke dip, and hearty bread brushed with olive oil, Paul opened the topic about the coins. "Let's recap what we know. They can't be in the original lighthouse lamp."

"Right," Glenys said. "But we know the pendants are a clue."

"And," Meranda added, "I believe they are in the lighthouse because of the box your family's pendant was kept in. It had a tin punch-art top with a picture of the lighthouse."

"Well, actually." Glenys chewed on her thumbnail. "I made that box in sixth grade and gave it to my dad for Father's Day. It was the year we bought the lighthouse."

"Okay." Strike that one. "Great job, by the way."

"Thank you." Glenys preened at the tongue-in-cheek compliment.

Jessie asked, "What about the plaques in the brick wall of the tower?"

Meranda pointed to her. "That's right. There is no doubt they're connected to the coins. So the pillars and the plaques all lead to the lighthouse." Her brain whirred. "Maybe instead of the clues leading up to the light, they lead down to the floor."

"Yeah." Jessie turned to Glenys. "Could they be under the floor?"

"No. The lighthouse underwent a major renovation a few decades ago. The entire floor was replaced. If they'd been there, I'm sure someone would have found them."

Meranda feared she had hit another brick wall. How many clues would it take to unearth the mystery?

"May I see your necklace?" Paul held out his hand to

Meranda. She unhooked the chain and passed it to him. He looked at the back again. "JG.IG." He squinted and looked at it again. "Wait a minute. . ."

Meranda, along with Glenys and Jessie, leaned forward. Derrick had disappeared. She assumed he'd gone below to use the latrine.

"What, Paul? What do you see?"

"Just a minute." He handed the necklace back, excused himself, and headed below.

A satisfying sensation prickled the back of Meranda's neck, signaling a breakthrough.

⁂

Paul jogged down the steps, but he nearly tripped over Derrick, who was bent over something near the refrigerator.

"I think we ate the last of the food. Are you getting another soda?"

"Um, yeah. Want one?"

As he stood, Paul saw him shove something into his pocket and try to shut the drawer that Meranda's purse was in, but the strap hung out, preventing him from doing so.

"Were you in Meranda's bag?" Then he noticed dollar bills sticking out of Derrick's pocket. "Are you stealing from her?"

"No way, dude." He shoved the money in deeper.

"Come on. Let's talk to Meranda." He propelled Derrick through the opening to the deck, but reached back for Meranda's bag before following. Had Derrick spotted Meranda's purse straps hanging out of the drawer and seized his opportunity?

Paul steered Derrick toward Meranda by pushing the back of his shoulder.

She looked up at both of them and squinted in the sun. Then her gaze dropped to the item in Paul's fist. "What are you doing with my bag?"

He handed it to her. "Check your money."

She hesitated a moment, but then complied. She pulled out her wallet, opened it, and frowned. "I had two hundred and fourteen dollars in here."

"I'll bet Derrick has two hundred and fourteen dollars in his left pocket."

"Derrick?" She held out her hand.

He rolled his eyes but reached in and pulled out the wad of bills. She counted them and glared at Derrick.

Jessie shot out of her chair. "Derrick, you idiot!"

Paul had never seen her so angry, her wrath making Derrick wither. Did he fear she might hit him? He shrank onto a seat on the deck.

Glenys joined Jessie in the verbal whipping. "Wait a minute. At my sister's wedding, you were the last one in the kitchen. I saw you go back in when the police arrived. Are you the one who took my dad's pendant?"

Derrick's gaze shot to Jessie.

Jessie stepped between them. "Of course he didn't. Why would he want your old pendant? He just went back into the kitchen to be sure we didn't leave anything." Was that the classic turnaround to protect her man when it looked like someone else might throttle him?

Paul held up his hand. "We'll turn him in when we get back and let the authorities figure out what happened."

Meranda nodded, and taking her bag with her, she stepped to the helm and grabbed her radio to report the incident.

Derrick sat with his arms crossed, scowling. "I didn't take the pendant."

"Maybe not," Paul said, "but you did take Meranda's money."

The boat engine roared to life, and before long they were underway.

thirteen

As Meranda chugged her boat to the dock, a patrol car and two men in uniform waited for them. Within the hour, she and the others had given their statements, with Glenys adamant the sheriff search Derrick's home for the pendant.

Blackhearted buzzard. There should be honor on a boat. She had never felt the need to lock up her belongings before.

The sheriff cuffed Derrick and placed him in the patrol car. Jessie stood nearby, pacing the parking lot and flinging her small duffel bag around her body as if she wanted to hit someone with it. By the daggers shooting from her eyes at her boyfriend, Meranda assumed Derrick would be the one sporting bruises. Finally, as the car pulled away, Jessie seemed to gain control and glanced toward the trio.

"I'm sorry he ruined our trip, everyone."

"Has he ever done anything like this before?" Paul asked, not in an unkind way.

"Do you think I'd be with him if he did?" She scowled and moved toward her car. "Again, I'm really sorry."

"Jess, wait." Paul followed her. "Are you going to be okay?"

Meranda also wondered if Jessie could use some company. She called out to her. "Yeah, Jessie. You're welcome to hang out here."

An angry frown slashed across her forehead. "No. I'd rather be alone right now. Thanks." Then she stormed off to her car, gunned the engine, and peeled out of the lot.

Meranda stood with Glenys behind Paul as he watched Jessie's car until it disappeared around a corner. Tension had drawn his shoulders up to squeeze his neck. She thought of rubbing those shoulders, but reached out to touch his arm instead. "I'm so sorry for Jessie. What will happen to Derrick now?"

"Probably a slap on the wrist for the money if it was his first offense. If they find the pendant, depending on its worth, he'll be in a whole lot more trouble." He frowned. "In any event, he's fired."

All three stood silent for a moment longer. Meranda glanced up and down the dock. The other boaters had gone back to their regular activities after the squad car left. A cop dragging someone from the Drake boat in handcuffs? That had to have confirmed in her neighbors' minds that the family was someone to avoid.

Finally she returned to the boat. "Party's over. Guess I'll clean up."

Paul followed. "I'll do the galley. Too bad there aren't any leftovers. I could leave them for you. Next time I'll make extra."

"I've got the trash," Glenys announced. When she was through collecting soda cans and tossing them into a trash bag, she dropped onto the bench with the drama of a 1920s actress in a Rudolph Valentino movie. "I was having so much fun with you guys. Does it have to end? I'll be going back to California soon."

"When?" Paul asked as he reappeared on deck.

"I start shooting a small indie film in a couple of weeks. You'll probably never see it." She dragged herself to stand. "I have twelve lines. One scene. I'm a waitress." She grimaced and snatched her purse that she'd laid on the deck. "I hated waitressing before I became an actress. And now I'm playing one in a movie." She moved to the back of the boat and, with Paul's help, hopped to the dock from the dive platform. "I don't even get to die in this movie. Just take someone's order, make a wisecrack, and step offstage." With a huge dramatic sigh, she turned and made her exit.

She didn't get far, however. A large pelican stood on the dock blocking her way. "Shoo! Shoo! Go away!" She stood a good twenty feet from it and gesticulated wildly to no avail. When it started hopping toward her and clicking its bill, she shrieked as she did during the seagull attack and ran back to the boat, leaped on board, and hid behind Paul.

The look of terror in her eyes finally got Meranda's attention. "You really are afraid of big birds."

"And little ones. And all of them in between."

"I understand fear," Paul said. "Let me walk you to your car."

She accepted with a sigh and allowed him to go first. He waved his arms at the pelican, and it spread its wide wings and flew away.

When she was gone, Paul returned to Meranda. "That poor girl. I can so relate." He stroked his chin. "I just had a thought. I don't know anything about acting, but I remember meeting a producer at my stepcousin's wedding in Oakley. His uncle, I believe. I think I'll ring up Skye and see if he can do anything to help Glenys."

Meranda nodded her approval while sweeping the deck. What a sweet guy. Everyday she learned more about this unassuming man. And she loved every facet of this treasure.

With the boat back to its original spit shine, Meranda sank onto the bench seat.

"You really surprised me, Paul." Meranda propped her elbow onto the back of the seat and leaned her head into her hand.

He joined her, sitting close enough their knees touched. "Why?"

"Getting your boating card? Isn't that a huge step for you?"

"I think we had it right. Once my nausea was conquered and I learned how to drive a boat, I lost my anxiety. It was as you said—all about control. I've had to deal with out-of-control issues all my life. My dad dying when I was young.

My single mom making difficult decisions that I had no say in. Then, of course, there's my grandmother—under her thumb until I moved inland just a few years ago. Since I've moved back, I realize how I really hate that."

"So you were projecting those control issues until they manifested under the guise of your fear."

He raised his eyebrow.

"College. Psych 101."

"Ah." He nodded. "I think so. And now that I've been through the online boating course, I feel that if something should happen to the captain, I'd be okay."

"So are you going to get your airplane pilot's license now?" Meranda cast a teasing glance his way.

A telltale sheen appeared on his upper lip. "No. I don't think so."

"Hey." She gently slapped his shoulder. "Not to change the subject, but you had a revelation before the Derrick thing but never got a chance to reveal it. What did you go below for?"

"Oh!" He hopped out of the chair and raced down the steps. When he returned, he had Augustus's journal. "Look at the inscription on your pendant."

She lifted the pendant from its chain around her neck, peering at the back. "JG.IG." What did the journal and the pendant have to do with each other?

He opened the journal to June 16. "Now, look at this date."

"Six, sixteen. So, what about it?"

"You don't see it?"

She studied the inscription and the date several times before the number six slapped her on the forehead. "It's the same."

"Right. Written in older script, the six resembles a *G*. And I think it's possible that's not an I, but a one. Not JG.IG, but J6.16."

She frowned. "It still couldn't be a date, could it?"

"What if it's scripture?"

"I suppose it could be."

Paul took the journal and began turning pages. "Augustus was a religious man. He quoted scripture often." He opened to a page where the author journaled about the numerous stars while on the same voyage with his bride. "Here he quotes Psalm 8:3–4. 'When I consider thy heavens, the work of thy fingers, the moon and the stars, which thou hast ordained; what is man, that thou art mindful of him? and the son of man, that thou visitest him?' Perhaps whoever scratched these letters and numbers was also a believer. Do you have a Bible?"

"Not on the boat, why?"

"How about your laptop? Do you have Internet while docked here? I can look up some verses to see if they hold any clues."

She always had her laptop with her, in case she might have a revelation and want to look something up. It was below in the same drawer as her bag. Could it really be scripture? That made sense. The journals and letters she'd read were written by people of faith. They often talked about God and quoted scripture. Then they signed off with *The Lord be with you* or something similar. When had her family stopped seeking the Lord?

Sitting down near Paul again, she handed him the computer. "Here you go."

He put it in his lap and turned it on. "I know of a Bible Web site that shows different versions. Your ancestors would have used the King James Version." He started clicking away, going through every book that began with a *J*, his face glowing as he read the verses aloud. Meranda thought about her ancestors and their faith. Faith had gotten them through some tough times according to what she'd read. Paul had faith in God, and it helped him through his mom's death.

Glenys had faith also. If they all had gotten it right, did that make her wrong?

"This one looks interesting." Paul pulled her from her reverie. " 'Thus saith the LORD, Stand ye in the ways, and see, and ask for the old paths, where is the good way, and walk therein, and ye shall find rest for your souls.' It's from Jeremiah 6:16."

Meranda watched a rainstorm gathering several miles off the coast. She doubted they were in the path. It looked to be going southeast.

"What do you think?"

"I don't know. How would it apply to the coins?"

"This part about the old paths. These coins have been on an old path leading from generations past."

She leaned over and read the scripture on the screen. "Well, if I find them, I'll sure get rest for my soul."

He clicked on the keyboard some more, and another screen appeared. "Here it is in a different version. Hmm. That's interesting."

"What?" She almost felt as if a magnet were drawing her in to read what was on the screen.

"This one talks about crossroads and ancient paths." He bookmarked the page, then shut the laptop and looked at her. "Even if this isn't the verse on the pendant, would you be open to thinking that the Lord may be speaking to you through this one?"

Had that been the magnetic pull? She felt the skin prickle on her neck. "So what are you saying?"

He paused a moment as if he was thinking about his next words. "You may be at a crossroads right now. You can either continue on this path, which may or may not lead to the coins, or you can stop, pray, and let God lead you."

"But He may not want me to find the coins." She leaned back and crossed her arms.

"Then, if that's true, that's the path you should choose because God wants what's best for you." He placed his arm on the back of the seat behind her, his face just inches from hers. "And so do I." Mahogany eyes bored into hers so deeply she felt them prick her heart.

While still a breath apart, he said, "Good night, Meranda. Know that I pray for you every day and will say a special prayer tonight." Then he was gone. Her lips tingled as if he had kissed her, and she felt a little miffed that he hadn't.

That night, the sheets tangled her legs as she tossed in bed, wrestling with whether she should give up and hand her dream—Pop's dream—over to God or fate or whatever it was called. No. As long as she was in control, she knew she'd find them eventually.

Control.

Paul conquered his fear by learning how to run a boat, taking control over it. Yet his grandmother used control the wrong way. Meranda searched her own soul.

Am I a control freak?

Possibly, but she wasn't going to give control over to a God who allowed her father to die.

Realizing sleep had abandoned her, she got up, slid into her clog slippers, and padded out to the living room. Without turning on the lights, she stood at the back window and watched the lighthouse.

Wink. Wink.

"What should I do, Pop? Paul says I should give our dream to God." Mom needed the money. Meranda needed to validate Pop. The coins would not materialize out of nowhere; she didn't care how powerful God was.

She flipped on the desk lamp, finding the letter written by Augustus, and poured over it—again. It never stated the coins were in his possession, just that they were where no one would find them. Were they in the wreckage?

An hour later, light started to filter through the window and with it an idea. As she prepared for her day, weary from the lack of sleep yet charged with adrenaline, she called Jessie.

"Hey, you mentioned you're a certified diver?"

fourteen

The next morning Paul sat in the restaurant office with Derrick's employee chart. He had just finished up the paperwork to terminate the thief.

"Pablo." His grandmother poked her head in the door.

"Morning, Abuelita. Come in, I need to tell you something."

He stood and offered her the desk chair in the cramped space. As he pointed out the chart, he told her about Derrick and their adventure the day prior.

"I never liked him." She molded her face into the bulldog look. "His eyes are too close together." Sometimes Abuelita didn't like someone because of eyes that were too far apart. Or an offset nose. Or teeth that were too straight.

"We'll have to hire someone to take his place." An idea struck him. "What about Meranda's sister? She's been through culinary school, but I think she may be open to filling in as waitstaff to get her foot in the door."

"I would need to look at her very closely. Check her credentials. I will set up the interview."

He threw his shoulders back and shed the years of control she had heaped on him. "No, Abuela." He rarely called her *grandmother,* and this got her attention. Her head snapped up. "This is my business. Our agreement was that you would retire. What happened to that?"

Abuelita pierced him with a glare. "You are getting too cocky for your own good, Pablito."

Paul slipped his hand under her elbow and removed her from his chair. "I'm not 'little Pablo' anymore. I'm a grown man who needs to run my business as I see fit. You gave this restaurant to Albert and me. Now trust us." He tenderly, but forcefully, ushered her out of the office.

Closing the door behind her, he heaved a sigh. Man, that felt good.

Now back to filling the gap Derrick's absence had caused. He wanted to talk to Meranda before offering her sister the job. Considering Rose's social position, he wasn't sure how receptive she would be. He sat at the desk and called Meranda's cell phone, but her voice mail picked up. She was probably on a charter tour.

He checked his calendar. He could fill in until Thursday if he didn't connect with Meranda before then. He had no catering jobs on that day, so a surprise visit to her boat might be fun. He left the office for an appointment to talk about food choices for a birthday party and nearly tripped over Abuelita, who was standing in the corridor gazing with misty eyes at a picture of his grandfather.

"Abuelita?" He stroked the thin shoulder. Had he pushed her too far?

"Sevilla."

"Excuse me?"

She turned moist gray brown eyes to him. "Your abuelo and I had often talked about going back to our home in Sevilla, España."

His stomach dropped. "Spain. I didn't mean for you to go away. I just want you to rest now. You and Papa did a wonderful job with this restaurant. But it's time for you to pass the torch."

She nodded and wiped a tear, frightening him. Abuelita rarely cried. He pulled her into a hug. "Are you okay?"

"You have never spoken to me like that before, Pablo." She looked up at him with flashing eyes. *Here comes the backlash.* "And you are right."

"I'm right?" His head spun with this sudden turnaround.

"Don't back down now, Pablo." She stroked his cheek with bony fingers. "You are so like your mother. I had to push her out of the nest, too. Of course she came back, but she brought you."

Paul chuckled and hugged the tiny body. "I love you, Abuelita."

She hugged him back, fierce twig arms that nearly busted his rib. Then she pulled back, a mischievous grin playing on her face. "Then I stay."

He turned her by the shoulders and gently directed her toward the door. "No, you go. Take up painting."

Thursday morning when he arrived at the dock, Meranda wasn't on the charter boat. He searched the dock and spotted her on the smaller *Romanda Jule*. She was busy with her preparations and didn't see him right away as he walked toward her. She had on a black wet suit, the upper half hanging at her waist to reveal a navy blue swimsuit. Knowing she enjoyed diving, this didn't surprise him. Her reaction to him, however, did.

"What are you doing here?" Her eyes shifted like she seemed distracted. She'd just released the rope from the dock.

"I'd like to ask you something about your sister and decided to surprise you."

Jessie suddenly appeared from below holding a pair of goggles. She was also dressed in a wet suit. "Hey, Meranda. What do you use to keep your mask from fogging? I've heard a cut potato works." She stopped in her tracks when she saw Paul. "What are you doing here?"

He jerked his hands into the air. "Why are you both so shocked that I'm here?"

"Because you should be at work." Jessie's voice held more impatience than Meranda's had. What was going on with these two? She tossed the mask with the attached snorkel toward a pile of neon yellow vests and a couple of scuba tanks near the diving platform.

"Are you going to the jetty for Dungeness crabs?"

Meranda avoided his eyes as she tossed the rope into the boat and boarded.

Paul's heart dropped to his stomach. "You're *not* going to dive the wreckage."

With her characteristic captain stance—legs planted firmly on the deck and hands on hips—Meranda challenged him. "Is that an order or an observation?"

He leaped onto the boat and rushed to Meranda, grabbing her shoulders. "I thought you were going to let God guide you. Surely you don't believe He's telling you to put yourself in danger."

She shrugged his hands away. "I'll be fine. I have to do this." She removed the pendant from her neck and placed it in her bag sitting on the deck near the steps. Then she stormed past him and took the helm.

"This is crazy!" He followed her up the steps and into the small space.

She turned to face him. "I know this shipwreck." Meranda ground her teeth. "I dove it with my father. Maybe if I had gone with him that last time. . ."

"Is this a guilt thing? You know you had nothing to do with his death."

"I know I wasn't there to help. I know our last conversation was an argument." She sat in the captain's chair, turning her back on him, and with a voice barely above a whisper said, "I know I called him crazy."

"You what?" Paul couldn't believe what he heard. She hated others calling him that.

Her shoulders had been squared, but at her confession they drooped slightly. With her back still to him, she said, "His funds had run out, but he took the boat out one last time with a minimal crew to look for the coins—on my birthday." She turned to look at Paul and beat her chest. "And I wanted to spend it with my whole family. But that morning he grabbed me by the shoulders, right here on this dock. The look in his eyes scared me. He said, 'I'm close, Bonnie-girl. So close.' And he left me standing there. No promises of coming in early for the dinner Rose had prepared. I felt I lost him right then. As he pulled away, I called out to him. I told him he was as crazy as everyone said he was. He never looked back at me. I don't even know if he heard me. But if he did. . ."

Her shoulders sagged even farther, but she placed her hand on the key and turned the engine over. "We had just lit the candles on my cake after waiting a couple of hours to see if he would show. That's when we got the phone call."

"And now you're acting just like him. How does that honor his memory?"

Without looking up, she snarled. "Either get off my boat or grab a vest and hang on because we're pulling out."

"I'll stay." Perhaps he could talk her out of it once they got there.

"No!" Jessie balled her fists. "Go home, Paul." When both he and Meranda turned shocked gazes toward her, she stammered, "I–I mean, this is ladies day out."

He looked back at Meranda, who shrugged. "Do what you want. But this boat is leaving in two seconds."

Should he leave? Something didn't feel right, and it was mostly a vibe he got from Jessie. But moreover, he hoped to talk Meranda out of diving the wreck. He sat and strapped himself in. Jessie slapped her chair before sitting in it.

He did have to hang on as the boat bounced on the water, bringing back his fear. *Lord, be with us. And be with Meranda if she attempts this stunt.*

Soon the boat spiraled to a stop like a teenager-driven car spinning a doughnut in a parking lot. The rumbling engine silenced, and the only sound was the water slapping at the hull.

Jessie had been sitting across from him during the rough ride, an ugly sneer on her face. She stood and grabbed one of the tanks, opened the valve, and sniffed it.

Paul removed his seat belt but had to sit a moment longer to quell his nauseous stomach. He wished he had his wristbands. Finally he stood and wobbled on land legs to try to confront her. "Jessie. You need to talk her out of this. Her father died down there. It can't be safe."

Jessie's glare shot venom. "I'm not at the restaurant right now. You can't order me here."

He staggered back from the verbal strike. "I know that. I'm asking as a friend."

"Move." She shoved him aside and grabbed a diving vest. "Meranda is a big girl. She's an experienced diver and knows this wreck. I'm certified with several shipwreck dives under my belt. Let her do this. Maybe she'll get some closure." She glanced down at Meranda's bag sitting near the steps, an almost yearning look passing across her face.

She then moved to the dive platform and dipped the vests into water while Meranda anchored the boat.

Paul watched helplessly as the two women slipped the vests over the tanks and helped each other put them on. He thought of calling the coast guard, but what could he tell them? His friends weren't doing anything illegal. He silently turned to the one Authority he knew he could count on, God, as Meranda's fins disappeared over the side.

When there was nothing left in the water but the bubbles from their tanks, he concentrated on the spot for an eternity, like a dog waiting for his owner to return. When his watch ticked by a slow half hour, another boat, a cabin cruiser like Meranda's, only smaller, was upon him before he knew it, startling him with its nearness. It came to a stop about twenty feet away. Derrick glowered at him from his place at the wheel.

"How did you get out of jail?" Paul clenched his fists, wishing he could get his hands on the twerp.

"Hey, dude. I didn't steal that pendant. The cops didn't find anything, so I got out on bail for the cash I stole. Just for the record, I've never done anything like that before."

Paul shook his head. So much failed to make sense. "Why are you here?"

"Jessie called this morning and told me to meet her out here. She didn't say *you'd* be here."

The two men held a staring standoff until a rubbery flopping sound on Derrick's boat caught their attention. Jessie had just tossed her fins onto the deck. She climbed up the ladder and stepped into the boat.

"Hey," Derrick spoke to her. "I couldn't do what you said with him there."

Not even looking at Paul, she ripped off her mask and shouted, "Shut up! Let's get out of here!" She tossed a book-sized object into a large canvas athletic bag. Then she proceeded to undo her gear, violently ripping the Velcro and shrugging out of the vest.

"Where's Meranda!" Cold fear iced Paul's nerve endings. He searched the water hoping to see her surface.

Jessie didn't answer him. While she sat with her back to Paul and slipped off her boots, he raced to the helm, radioed the coast guard, and managed to stammer that he thought his friend was hurt in a diving accident and that there could have been foul play.

"What's your location?"

"I don't know." He searched the console, hoping to see something with numbers. "Um. . ." He shook his head to clear it. "We're above the wreckage of the *Victoria Jane*."

"Got it. We're on the way." Paul broke off before asking how long it would be. He ran back to the deck, nearly stumbling as the boat rocked beneath him. The engine of the other boat cranked a couple of times, but then nothing.

"Come on!" Jessie's voice graveled frustration.

"It won't start." Fear showed on Derrick's face as he struggled to start the boat. Whatever could he be afraid of?

Jessie reached into a compartment on board and pulled out a gun, pointing it at Paul. Now he understood. Derrick knew what Jessie was capable of.

"Jessie!" Panic seized his feet, but where could he run? "What are you doing? Don't be stupid."

She kept her eye on Paul but barked at Derrick. "Get on Meranda's boat. Bring it over here."

"But I don't have my swim trunks on."

She rolled her eyes. "Then you should have gotten closer. I don't care if you have to strip to your Skivvies. Just get over there." She flicked the end of the pistol toward him. "Remember who bailed you out."

Grumbling, he removed his tennis shoes and looked like he might consider throwing them into Meranda's boat, but must have thought better of it. He lowered himself, jeans and all, down the ladder while holding the shoes high and inhaled sharply as the cold water soaked into his clothes.

By the time he reached the *Romanda Jule,* his shoes had taken several dunkings. He struggled up the ladder in his heavy clothes and paused to rest on the dive platform.

"Hurry up!" Jessie stamped her foot. Derrick shot daggers with his glare but stood and walked to the helm, leaving large puddles of water on the deck.

With the gun trained on both of them, Paul knew he couldn't do anything to stop Derrick, so he let him pass. Derrick climbed the steps, started the boat, and swung it around to get close to the other vessel.

"Closer, you idiot!" Jessie stood at the side, her wet suit gone and wearing a two-piece swimsuit splashed with orange flowers. She flung her duffel bag over her shoulder.

"This is as close as I can get," Derrick roared loud enough for her to hear on the other boat. "You want me to bump into you?"

"Whatever. Just throw me the rope."

He rushed past Paul on his way to the dive platform. Derrick threw the rope to Jessie and she pulled until the boats bumped together. When Derrick held out his hand to help transfer her to Meranda's boat, a rogue wave rolled under both boats at that moment. Jessie yelped and ended up in the water.

Derrick, however, ended up with the gun. His wide eyes suggested he had no idea his day would include boat hijacking.

Paul's mind spun. These were real-life pirates! "Derrick, put the gun down. She's obviously insane." Derrick turned a stunned look toward him.

With Jessie still thrashing in the water, struggling to throw her bag on board, Paul rushed the larger man. He had to overpower him before Jessie made it on board. They wrestled, Derrick throwing Paul down onto the deck like a dockworker with a sack of potatoes. Paul kicked Derrick's ankles, sweeping his feet out from under him. He landed hard, and the gun went skittering. They both groped for it.

"Get it!" Jessie's voice sounded close, and Paul knew she was on board.

Paul's fingers claimed the weapon seconds before Jessie. He scrambled to stand, training it on her with trembling hands while keeping an eye on Derrick, still sitting on the deck and holding his head. Blood oozed from a gash in the back. He must have hit his head on the metal cleat in the deck where the rope had been moments before.

Jessie smirked, her lips an ugly slash. With her bag slung over her shoulder, she turned her back on him, snatched the pendant out of Meranda's bag, and ascended the steps to the helm.

"Stop, Jessie."

"Or what? You'll shoot?" She sat, again with her back to him, and turned over the engine easily. "We both know you won't do that."

"No, but *I* will."

Paul turned at the sound of the female voice. "Meranda?"

She stepped, finless, toward Paul and took the gun. With a steady hand, she held her arm straight in Jessie's direction. "Now, step away."

fifteen

Meranda aimed at her ex-friend's spine. Jessie raised her hands and moved slowly away from the wheel.

"What did you do with the slate, Jessie?"

When she didn't answer, Paul said, "She tossed some things into the bag she brought aboard. She took it with her up to the helm."

"Turn around, Jessie, and move down here to the deck."

She complied, her eyes two glowering orbs.

Paul raced up the steps. "I called the coast guard." He retrieved the bag. "What's in here?"

"Proof that my father was murdered." She glanced his way while still training the gun on Jessie. "Open it."

Paul unzipped the athletic bag. "What am I looking for?"

"An underwater writing slate, about the size of an address book."

"How could it have been there so long? Wouldn't the writing have faded?"

"No, we use a special pen that scratches the surface. It takes something abrasive to erase it."

Paul straightened, holding the slate over his head. "Got it!"

"Read what's inside."

He flipped open the cover and perused it briefly, then his eyes went wide. "What does this mean?"

"It means that Jessie's father murdered mine. Pop wrote that message on there." She motioned with the gun for Jessie to join Derrick on the deck floor. As she shrugged the tank off, she continued speaking to Paul. "It says, 'Kingston killing me.' How did he do it, Jess? Did he tamper with the guide string? Created a silt storm to disorient my father? Waited until his air ran out before he told anybody?"

"No! My dad tried to save yours. He returned to the boat for fresh tanks. He told the other member of the team to call the coast guard, then went back down. He acted heroically, but it was too late."

Paul still knelt by the bag and rubbed his neck. "Jessie could be right, Meranda. Maybe your dad just thought there was foul play."

"Then why did she just try to do the same thing to me? The acorn doesn't fall far from the tree, does it, Jessie?"

Meranda retrieved a rectangular object from a bag hanging from her belt. "I have a feeling the proof is in here. It's my dad's underwater digital camera. I've heard stories of divers losing their cameras for months and when they retrieved them, found the pictures as good as new. I'm sure my dad hid it from Kingston, knowing someone would find it eventually." She shot a look at Jessie. "I found it in the hole where the slate was, just before I was caught in a silt storm that she generated. Jessie took the spool of string with her so she could get out, but I couldn't see. Luckily, I had found his camera in the hole in the floor before all that happened."

Paul stood and joined Meranda. "Jess, how could you?" His voice held a hard edge. Meranda knew he was no doubt hurt and confused by the turn of events.

Jessie shot a defiant glare at Paul. "You don't believe her, do you? She's so obsessed over the coins she'd lie to cover her own insanity. You know me, Paul. Why would I hurt her?"

"For the same reason you would pull a gun on me, I suppose." He wrapped his arm around Meranda's waist. She leaned into him, grateful for both his physical and mental support. He could have believed his assistant whom he'd known much longer.

A coast guard ship approached from the distance. "We'll let

the authorities sort it out. By the way, she has your pendant."

A half hour later, an officer loaded Jessie and Derrick onto the coast guard craft in handcuffs. Meranda turned the slate and the camera over as evidence and told them what Jessie had said about her father claiming to be a hero.

Derrick began singing his innocence, insisting that Jessie had told him to come and steal the pendant while the two were diving. "I'm not going down for another one, Jessie!"

"Another one?" Meranda looked at Paul.

He called out to the officer who handcuffed Jessie. "You might check her for an important artifact taken from Judge Bernard's house."

The officer gave him a thumbs-up as they sped away.

Meanwhile, another officer stayed on Meranda's boat and insisted on medically checking her.

"I'm fine."

Paul sat near enough that she could feel his support, but out of the way. "Sit down and let the nice man do his job."

She glanced his way, and while his eyes twinkled a teasing message, they also telegraphed that he'd help her sit if she didn't on her own.

With her seated, the officer checked her vitals. "How fast did you rise to the surface?"

"As fast as I could, but I tried to regulate it."

"Are you experiencing any fatigue, itching of the skin, stiffness in the joints, numbness, or shortness of breath?"

Blast! All she needed was the bends on top of nearly becoming fish food. She shook her head and wondered if they were checking Jessie for the same thing.

"Why are you rubbing your arm?"

"It's sore here." She indicated the fleshy part of her upper arm. "Probably from trying to get out. I had to squeeze through a hole."

"You want to tell me about that, ma'am?"

As she related her underwater adventure, she kept an eye on Paul. He seemed to suffer along with her.

She and Jessie had found the entrance into the skin of the ship. They tied off their line so they could make it back out. "I had been in there several times, so I knew where to go." They found the cabin, and Meranda saw the hole in the floor. It didn't go straight through to the lower compartment, but only to a subfloor. Meranda started moving debris from the hole, sure this was where Pop had left off before his death. Her hand felt the hard plastic casing of the camera, and she pulled it out and placed it into her bag.

"Divers lose things all the time," she told Paul. "It didn't surprise me that his camera would have fallen into the hole."

What did surprise her, however, was the slate.

"Pop's writing slate was also in the hole. Jessie was right there watching as I pulled it out. We both saw what he had written at the same time, and that's when we both knew. Her father had killed mine." She swallowed the new grief so she could go on. "Jessie grabbed the slate and moved to the guide string. She started kicking up silt until I became disoriented. Then Jessie followed the string out—taking the spool with her—leaving me to fend for myself. I couldn't find the door, so I dropped and searched the floor for the hole. I knew there was a way out from the compartment below. When I found the hole, I took off my tank and smashed through the subfloor. As I squeezed through, I strained my arm." She rubbed her upper arm, feeling like it might fall off. "Luckily, there was better visibility below. The jagged hole in the hull allowed light to filter in, so I headed toward it and out to safety."

The officer put away his equipment and smiled, perhaps for the first time since arriving. "You're one lucky lady. Let us know if you feel any of the symptoms I just mentioned. I'm concerned about the arm. We'll sling it, but I'm also putting you on oxygen and an IV just as a precaution. We don't want to mess with decompression sickness. We'll have an ambulance waiting for you at the dock."

"I don't need an ambulance."

"Yes, you do," Paul piped in. "I'll go with you."

Paul drove the boat back but needed some help from the officer to maneuver it into the slip.

In the ambulance, Paul sat next to her holding her hand. "You were awesome on the boat."

She smiled and lifted the oxygen mask just a little so she could talk. "By what I saw, you were holding your own with those two."

His chest puffed. "Yeah, well. . .you watch enough cop shows, you learn a few things. I didn't intimidate Jessie, though."

She patted his hand. "That's okay. We made a good team."

"That's right. We've got each others' backs." His eyes suddenly sparkled. "Oh, that reminds me why I showed up this morning. With Derrick fired"—he tilted his head—"and now with Jessie gone, I need some help at the restaurant."

Meranda pointed to her chest and raised her eyebrows.

"Good grief, no! I'm not asking you. If I ever need someone to make Twinkies and peanut butter sandwiches, though, you're my girl." He gently chucked her chin. "I was thinking of your sister."

"Rose?" She raised her thumb in approval. "You're her new role model."

"At first I was going to ask her to fill in for Derrick, but now I need a good sous chef. I didn't know if I should approach her about it, given your family's social status."

"Ask her. She'll be thrilled."

The tech inside the ambulance put a stop to her talking by putting the oxygen mask back in place, and they pulled into the emergency entrance of Crossroads Bay Medical Center.

ॐ

She was wheeled into a room that had been partitioned off

with curtains and transferred to a bed. Moans of several patients in various stages of distress reached her ears. As people came in and out, she tried to convince each one that she felt fine.

A woman doctor with spiky bleached hair finally came in and after an examination said, "I'd like to keep you here for just a few more hours."

"I don't have the bends." Meranda rolled her eyes, but then realized she had a dull headache. Probably from the stress of the day. Or too much oxygen.

The doctor regarded her with patience, as if she dealt with people all day long who knew their own bodies. "You don't seem to have DCS, but why take chances? I'm sure you'll be going home soon."

At least she didn't have to sit in a decompression chamber. She hated those things.

She asked if she could have visitors—Paul had been told to stay in the waiting room while they settled her in—and when she was told she could, she expected him to appear from behind the curtain. Instead her mother trotted in.

"Meranda! Are you okay? Are you hurting anywhere? I am so angry with you. Let me know if you need anything."

"Whoa, Mom. Lots of emotion there for me to weed through with my aching head."

"I'm sorry." She lowered her voice to just above a whisper. "I'll go tell them you're in pain."

"No, I can't have anything yet until they're sure I don't have the bends. An analgesic will just mask the symptoms." She patted the bed. "Come here. Sit with me."

Mom lowered herself to the bed, her shoulders slumped, tears threatening to spill from red-rimmed eyes that had probably already done their share of crying for the day. Meranda recognized this behavior. She'd seen plenty of it in the days after Pop's accident.

She reached out for her mother's hand. "I'm sorry."

Mom gripped the fingers in between her palms. "What were you thinking? What was your father thinking?"

"I know, Mom, you were right." This stopped her mother in midargument. "Dad was foolish to attempt to find the coins in such a dangerous place. When I thought I might join him in his watery grave, all I could think about was you, Rose, and Julianne. How losing one more to the coins would be devastating to you. Please forgive me for my selfishness."

Mom swept a curl from Meranda's brow. "You're so like your father." She spoke with a tenderness Meranda had never heard before.

"Is that a good thing, Mom?"

"I'm beginning to think it is." Her sigh bordered on exasperation. "My little adventurer. When Paul called to tell me they were bringing you to the hospital—and why—I was livid. But as I drove here, I realized this is who you are. You have your father's blood running hot in your veins. I can't change you. . .nor would I want to."

Meranda allowed the words to wash over her. She hadn't realized how much she needed her mother to understand her. "Thanks, Mom."

"And did you find the coins?"

"No, but I found Pop's camera." She shared what had happened between her and Jessie. "I turned it in to the coast guard. There will be an investigation."

Mom covered her face with one hand while holding onto Meranda's with the other. "I hate to live his death all over again, but I'll do what I have to do." The squeeze she gave to Meranda's fingers translated to a desperate clinging.

"We, Mom. We're in this together." She would not abandon her mother again.

"May we come in?" Rose and Julianne stood at the opening to the curtain.

"Of course." She opened her arms and both women flew into the cubicle, but only gently attacked her in hugs and kisses. "Where have you been?"

"In the waiting room with Paul." Julianne plopped into the only chair. "He suggested letting Mom come in first. Besides, she wanted to throttle you in private." After a glare from their mother, she added, "That's what you said."

"Well, the throttling is over." Mom patted Meranda's hip.

Meranda turned back to Rose. "Did you talk to Paul? He has a job offer."

Her sister's eyes lit up. "Yes, he told me about it."

"I know it will help pay for the wedding." She looked back at their mother. "I'm sorry, Mom. But we know you're in trouble."

Her mother nodded and dropped her gaze to her hands.

Meranda turned back to Rose. "I don't know how your fiancé will feel about you having a job, though."

"That isn't a concern anymore. We broke up."

"What? When?"

"This morning. I realized I didn't love him. Mom and I talked."

"She confronted me last night," Mom said. "She told me she didn't love him and that I was pushing the marriage. Honestly, I didn't know I was. He came from a good family, and I knew he would provide. But once she laid it out, I could see neither of them loved each other. Once he finds out we've lost our money, I'm sure he'll move on. Social climbers are like that."

It took one to know one. Meranda bit her tongue. None of that mattered now.

They stayed and chatted for a few more minutes. Finally Mom said, "Well, I know a young man who is probably pacing the floor out there. We'll go and let him sit with you."

She kissed Meranda on the forehead. Meranda couldn't

remember when she'd done that last. Tears stung her eyes as she watched her family leave.

A nurse about ten years her senior poked her head in. "I have someone out here looking for you. If you don't want him, I'm sure someone out here will snatch him up."

"Send him in." Her heart began to flutter, and she hoped they wouldn't keep her for hypertension. "Oh, and by the way, I'm fine. I shouldn't even be here."

"Yes you should." Paul stepped in as the nurse turned to leave, his arms folded and looking absolutely gorgeous in his protective mode.

Meranda felt that pleasant minnow sensation again, only this time it felt like they were chasing each other in a game of tag. She liked someone taking care of her. Who knew? He walked into the room and stood by the bed, taking her hand.

❧

Paul relished the feel of Meranda's hand in his. He tried to memorize every line, every knuckle as his fingers explored. Common sense continued to remind him to maintain only a friendship since he didn't want to be unequally yoked, but nearly losing this special friend had frightened him.

Meranda turned his wrist so she could see his watch. She gasped. "I had no idea it was almost evening. Do you have the dinner shift tonight?"

"No. I called Al, and he pulled someone in. Right now you're my priority." He settled into the chair near the bed.

"Paul, I need to tell you what happened down there."

He frowned, confused. "But I was listening when you told the coast guard."

"No, I need to tell you what happened in here." She pointed to her heart.

He leaned forward, eager to hear this story.

"After Jessie left, I was so alone. It was dark; I didn't know where the door was. . ." Her wide eyes reflected the terror she must have felt. "I was scared."

Shifting to the bed, he gathered her in his arms. Soft sobbing tore at his heart. He knew Meranda rarely, if ever, let people see this side of her. And he felt grateful that she chose him to show her vulnerability.

"Shh, it's okay now." He rocked her, letting her purge her emotions so she could talk.

Finally, she let go of his neck and sank back onto the pillow. "I thought I was going to join my dad. I wasn't ready to die."

"And I'm not ready to lose you." He smoothed her bedraggled hair from her wet face, thinking that even splotchy, she was the most beautiful woman he'd ever seen.

"While I was looking for the door, I prayed."

"You prayed?" *Thank You, Lord.*

"I thought about what you said. That I'm at a crossroads. When I chose to do this dive, I chose the path that leads to death. When I couldn't find the guide string, I thought about my dad and how he died the same way." Her sad eyes turned perplexed. "Then a strange thing happened. While I was thinking 'I've got to get out,' I heard in my head, 'Down.' It was then I remembered that the lower hold was accessible from the outside. Somehow I went right to the hole in the floor. I took off my tank and used it to smash through the subfloor. It wasn't hard to do, and I think Pop had the same idea. The wood splintered easily, as if it had only a few more good whacks to go. It's as if Pop saved my life." Her gaze turned back to Paul.

"Sounds like a miracle to me."

"I realized something else." She reached for his hand and gripped it tight. "I don't want to die not knowing Jesus as you and Augustus and Glenys know Him."

Paul's heart overflowed with praise. He cradled her hand with both of his and shared how all have fallen short of God's grace, how Christ died for her sins, and how all she had to do was accept God's free gift of salvation.

She closed her eyes and, gripping his hand, poured out her heart to the One who guided her out of the murky depths, both literally and spiritually.

When they were through, she seemed perplexed. "That's it?"

"That's it. The hardest thing is realizing you need a Savior. Asking Him into your heart is easy."

"Hm. I think I should work on my mom and sisters now."

Paul laughed and kissed the knuckles on her right hand. "So, you're back at that crossroads. What are you going to do now?"

"Give it to God. The coins aren't worth my life, and they weren't worth my dad's life. I'm through looking for the coins."

"I know that's what you're saying, and I know this latest search scared you, but are you sure you want to give up totally?"

She seemed to give his question some thought. A few seconds passed, and she thrust out her chin as if determined to live by her newfound faith. "If God wants me to find them, He'll show me the steps to take."

"What about your family?" One more test for her. It was one thing to trust God for one's own needs, but what about her loved ones?

"God will take care of my family."

"Yes, He will." He stood and leaned down to kiss her. "And we'll both take care of you."

sixteen

"Pablo."

"Yes, Abuelita." Paul sat in the office finishing Rose's paperwork after hiring her and showing her around the kitchen that morning. With her scores at the culinary institute and the test dishes he had asked her to prepare, he knew she would make a good fit. She left with promises to be back early the next morning.

Abuelita smiled. "I like her."

Paul raised an eyebrow. "Really? Even though you didn't get to interrogate her?"

"Do not be smart with me." She pulled the bulldog face but left the twinkle in her eye. "I have my ticket. I will see my sister in Sevilla, España, next week."

This news sucker punched him in the belly. "I thought you were kidding about that!" He didn't want her to move to another country, just out of the restaurant business. "I'll miss you, my abuelita." He stood and hugged her close, a lump the size of Spain in his throat.

He felt her chuckling near his chest. She reared her head and looked at his face. "I'll only be gone a month. Maybe I'll find new recipes for us to use, sí?"

He pulled her close again and cuddled her stick body. "I love you, Abuelita. Thank you for giving me this chance."

"You have earned it, Pablito." Her hand flew to her mouth. "Oops! I mean *big* Pablo. Your abuelo would be so proud."

Al poked his head in. "Are you still here? I thought you had a date with a boat captain."

Paul checked his watch. "Gotta run."

He kissed Abuelita on her head.

"Pablo. Where are you going?"

"It's my day off. Tomorrow we'll plan your going-away party, sí?"

Her eyes twinkled. "Sí." Then she wandered toward the kitchen where he heard, "Alberto."

Paul shook his head. Not even an entire ocean between them could keep Abuelita from trying to run her kitchen.

He grabbed his keys off the desk and hustled out the door. Meranda waited on her front porch for him, and he drove her to the lighthouse property.

"I'm so happy that Glenys invited us before she goes back to California." It had been a few days since Meranda's scare. Paul thanked God that her injuries weren't more severe. A strained arm was all her adventure into the abyss had cost her. And it seemed fine now with her bouncing in her seat in anticipation of seeing the lighthouse again.

"And she said she had a surprise for you."

"Yes." Her eyes widened into gray green saucers. "Maybe she found the coins!"

"Well"—he turned onto the lighthouse road—"I wouldn't get my hopes up. She didn't sound that excited."

They stopped at the gate. Paul rang the buzzer, identified himself, and the gate slid open.

"I really like that!" Meranda said. "No more closed doors around here."

They parked in front of the house, and the judge met them there.

"Uh-oh." Meranda slowly opened her door. "I hope it's okay if we're here."

His wave and smile seemed friendly enough to Paul.

After shaking their hands, the judge opened the conversation. "I want to let you know how sorry I am. Glenys told me about your. . .uh. . .adventure, and I can see now how important finding your family's treasure is to you. You're welcome to the lighthouse anytime. I give you my permission to look around."

Meranda smiled and thanked him, but then said, "My father died looking for the coins. Why wouldn't you think they'd be important to me?"

"The lighthouse property is just my vacation home. I didn't know about your father. Glenys has been quick to inform me, however." He scratched his ear and chuckled.

Interesting. The judge had an Achilles' heel.

"Glenys is in the lighthouse if you'd like to join her."

Meranda bounded up the slope toward the lighthouse but stopped abruptly and turned. "Thank you for opening your home to us."

The judge laughed. "You're welcome. Now go." He waved her off.

She swiveled and sprinted up the path to the lighthouse, leaving Paul to scurry behind.

When they entered, a *chink, chink* sound greeted them. Meranda put a foot on the first step and called up the winding staircase. "Glenys? You here?"

"Come on up."

They found her about three-quarters of the way up the winding staircase, chiseling away at one of the plaques on the wall.

"Glenys!" Meranda grabbed the little hammer out of her hand. "Your dad will be furious."

"Relax." Glenys snatched it back. "Dad said I could pry off one plaque if I didn't make a mess and could put it back exactly the same way. If there's something behind here, it shouldn't be hard to remove it."

Meranda scooted past her to sit on the top step, and Paul stayed below Glenys, impressed by her precision with the hammer and chisel. "Where did you learn to do that so neatly?"

"I had a bit part in a movie about an archeological dig."
She glanced down at him. "I doubt if you saw it."

"You know, Glenys," Meranda said as she played with the
pendant around her neck. "I don't feel the need to find the
coins anymore."

Glenys continued to chisel.

"Paul showed me that before my dive I was at a crossroads
with the coins. He shared a verse. 'Stand at the crossroads
and look; ask for the ancient paths, ask where the good way
is, and walk in it, and you will find rest for your souls.'"

Impressive that she could quote it without looking. She
must have gone back to the bookmarked site on her laptop
and thought a lot about their discussion.

"One path led to near destruction," she continued while
twirling the pendant around the tip of her finger. "The other
allows God to lead me if He thinks I should have the coins."

Chink. Chink. Glenys continued to work. Finally she said,
"I'm happy you've found peace with the coins. I believe God
will guide you, but now you've got me curious." *Chink. Chink.*
"If you don't mind, I'll keep looking until I leave."

"I'm curious, too," Paul said. "From the first time I saw the
pillars outside."

"May I see your pendant again, Meranda?" Glenys set aside
the hammer and chisel. "I didn't get a good look at it the
other day. Do the pillars outside really look like the image?"

"They do. Someone worked hard at crafting them." Meranda
unclasped the chain, but as she handed it down, Glenys only
grasped one side of the chain. The pendant slipped off the
necklace and began rolling down the steps like an errant tire
on the highway, creating a chorus of echoing clinks.

"Oh! I'm sorry!" Glenys started after it, but Paul stopped her.

"I'll get it." Paul grabbed the rail and hustled down the
steps. The pendant didn't stop until it hit the solid floor and
then rolled behind the open iron staircase. "Found it!" He

squatted to pick it up and heard more chiseling above. "It's fine. Not a mark on it."

Glenys's chiseling stopped, and he heard her squeal. He called up to her. "Did you find something?"

A pause. "No, just brick behind here."

"Too bad." Before heading back up, a number etched on the back of one of the steps caught his eye. Upon further inspection, he saw other numbers, but not on every step. Each was a different number going up in succession with every higher step. He peered through the staircase and saw that within his vision the steps with numbers coincided with a plaque.

"Hey, ladies." He pulled out the notebook he kept in his pocket for recipe ideas and jotted down the numbers. "You might want to see this."

Their feet pattered on the metal staircase. Handing Meranda's pendant back to her, he pointed to a number, then to the plaque.

Meranda slipped the chain back through the hole in the pendant and put it back on. She looked at Glenys. "Do you understand what that means?"

Glenys shook her head.

Paul fingered the number on the seventh step up, about his eye level. "Could be the order of the stairs so they would be assembled correctly."

Meranda bent down to look at the first number on the second step. "Then why does this have the number one?" They all inspected further. The next step with a number was the fifth one, but it had a number three. And so on up the staircase.

"Do either of you have a compact?" Paul asked.

Meranda looked at him as if he'd lost his mind. "I don't even wear makeup."

"I have one," Glenys said. "It's in the house, though. I'll run and get it."

While she was gone, Paul and Meranda stood under the staircase looking at the numbers.

"They don't seem factory etched." Meranda rubbed her fingers across one of the numbers. "Wouldn't it look a little more professionally done even a hundred years ago?"

Paul reached out and touched the number, brushing Meranda's hand. He glanced around the small space and noted her nearness. He wove his fingers between hers, and she swung her gaze to meet his. He praised God silently that this woman to whom he was attracted from the first meeting now shared his faith.

"I'm very glad you picked this crossroad, Meranda. Because it brought us here." With his other arm, he reached around her and drew her close. She leaned into his kiss, her full lips soft and warm. When they parted, he searched her gray eyes. "I don't know what I'd have done if I'd lost you the other day. I wouldn't have gotten the chance to tell you how I feel."

She reached around his neck. "And how do you feel?"

"I love you." He captured her mouth once more. Never in his life had he felt this kind of emotion. He had never been truly in love before. He wanted to protect this powerful sea captain with all his might, but more than that, he wanted to spend the rest of his life with her.

When he allowed her to speak, her words did not disappoint. "I love you, too." She tickled the back of his neck as she played with the strands of his hair. At that moment his whole world came into alignment.

"You can thank your grandmother."

He pulled back. "My grandmother?" He didn't need that image at this moment.

"Remember? The alcove, the candle, the soft music?"

Ah, yes. The first day she visited the restaurant. When he came out of the kitchen that day, his legs nearly buckled when he saw her. Gone was the pirate scarf, allowing her hair to float in soft red curls around her face. Like now. He wound a ringlet around his finger. "I remember."

"Wow. I leave for a second. . ." Glenys stood inside the door with a mischievous grin playing on her face.

"You could have taken your time," Paul told her.

"You need to let me know these things. A signal or something would have been helpful."

Paul held out his hand. "You have the mirror?"

She placed an odd-looking contraption into his palm. "This is what my dad uses on his cars when he needs to see something buried under the hood. I ran into the house and told him what we've found. He suggested this."

Paul handed Meranda his notebook. "Please jot down the numbers as I call them out." He took the round mirror by the handle and adjusted the swivel, then headed up the stairs. At each plaque, he slipped the mirror between the corresponding steps. "Six," he called down, then moved to the next plaque and step. "Eight." And the next. "Nine."

The judge entered as Paul called down the last numbers. Glenys showed him what they'd found.

"Wish I could help," he said. "I didn't even know the numbers were there. Looks to me like a combination to something."

Paul bounced down the stairs to join them. "Like a safe?"

Meranda cocked her head. "Aren't there too many numbers for that?"

"Probably." The judge scratched his chin. "Could be the numbers add up to something. Why don't we go in the house and brainstorm."

Glenys led the way out. "I'll make sandwiches. It's almost noon."

⁂

After lunch they all lingered around the kitchen table. Meranda wondered what Paul thought of Glenys's turkey sandwiches. They were good, but very plain.

Judge Bernard stood and cleared the plates. "Would you like to see some pictures of the property as they were building?"

"Are they the same ones as in the museum?" Meranda sipped her second cup of hot coffee, careful not to burn her tongue.

"Some are. These are the originals, the ones the photographer used to put in the paper. I found them in a box in the attic." He left to get them. When he came back, he laid a black photo album on the table.

"These are clearer." Meranda and Paul looked together. The album chronicled the building of the lighthouse from the ground breaking to finished product. Besides the fascination of the process, Meranda paid close attention to Augustus in the photos. What a jovial man he seemed to be. The museum pictures didn't show this side of him. He was laughing in several of the pictures, shaking hands with the mason near a pile of bricks, showing a group of men in suits the partial product, beaming from ear to ear as he stood in front of the finished lighthouse.

She flipped the page. A large house-sized hole had been dug and boards formed somewhat of a structure. "Is this the construction of the house?"

"Yes," the judge said. "There aren't as many because it wasn't as interesting, I suppose."

The final picture in the album was of Augustus leaning against a sign and standing where the road split off. The right going to the house and the left to the lighthouse. Both structures showed in the background.

Meranda squinted. "Is this a homemade street sign?" She never noticed it in the museum pictures. An unobtrusive wooden two-by-four had been staked into the ground with two rustic planks nailed onto it. "Those look like ship planks."

The judge swiveled the album toward him. "I haven't

looked too closely at this picture, but I believe you're right. Probably from the shipwreck."

Paul leaned in. "What's painted on them?"

Four heads pressed in on one another.

"Lighthouse Road and *something* Way," Meranda said. The first word was hard to see in the old photograph due to the angle.

"Starts with a *G*," Glenys contributed. "G–o–o—"

"Good!" Paul piped in.

Meranda frowned at him. "What's so good about it? We can't read it."

"No, that's the word. Good. Good Way." He tapped the table in his excitement. "What was the scripture you quoted to Glenys in the lighthouse?"

"Stand at the crossroads and look; ask for the ancient paths, ask where the good way is. . ." Her jaw dropped. "Good way! The coins are here in the house!"

seventeen

"Okay, let's think about this." Meranda leaned her elbows on the table, squeezed her eyes shut, and went over all the clues. "Augustus's letter led me to the property. The pendant led me to the pillars and confirmed we were on the right track. The pillars led me to the lighthouse. Inside the lighthouse, the plaques led to the steps and their numbers. If I hadn't been clumsy and dropped my pendant, we might never have gotten this far."

"I think that was God," Paul said.

"What? He slid it off the chain?"

"You were telling Glenys about the scripture and what you'd learned. I think God honored your obedience to give the search to Him."

Meranda's heart warmed to this. Even though she was new at letting God captain her life, she felt peace that Paul was right.

"So," she continued. "The steps and the numbers are no doubt important."

"I just remembered something." The judge pointed to the photograph showing the homemade road sign. "This picture hung in the lighthouse until the renovation, just above the highest plaque."

"Cool!" Glenys stabbed the air with her finger, drawing an imaginary line upward. "The steps and their numbers were supposed to lead to the photo, which told us the treasure is in the house somewhere." She frowned. "But where? Alison and I have been all over this place. As kids we found every nook and cranny. If the coins are here, they must be inside a wall or under a floor."

Meranda cocked an eyebrow at the judge.

"Oh no," he said, waving his arms. "You aren't tearing this place apart."

"We shouldn't have to tear the *whole* place apart." She shut her eyes again. "The pillars led to the lighthouse. The lighthouse led to the plaques. The plaques led to the steps. The steps led to the photo. The photo led to the house." *Think.* She paused in her brainsqueezing to pray. *Lord, You led me this far. Please show me the rest of the way.* She went through the entire sequence again in her head.

As if God turned on a spotlight, she saw the steps and their numbers in her mind. Her eyes popped open. "Steps!"

Now everybody's eyes were wide. Together they repeated. "Steps!"

"Let me see your notebook." Meranda held her hand out to Paul.

She took it and raced to the staircase leading to the bedrooms on the second floor.

"The numbers are one, three, six, eight, and nine." She counted the steps in the narrow stairway. Ten.

With the judge's nodding approval, she took Glenys's hammer and chisel and pried the board away from the first step. As light flooded the dark three-foot by one-foot space, her heart thudded a drumming beat in her ears.

Nothing.

She pried the third step.

Still nothing.

What could she have missed? *God, why would You have brought me this far only to fail?*

She sat on the second step, one that didn't have a corresponding number, with her head drooped into her hands. Hot, unshed tears stung her closed eyelids. Rubbing her face and fingering her hair out of her eyes, she addressed the three silent members of the search party. "Is there any way they could have been here and someone found them?"

The judge shrugged. "I suppose that's possible. Although I was assured when I bought this place that everything was original to the house."

"Wait." Paul tapped his temples, obviously taxing his brain as much as Meranda was hers. "Do you have Augustus's letter with you?"

She felt gooseflesh on the back of her neck and quickly retrieved it from her bag. They both skimmed it, looking for another clue.

"Yes!" Paul removed the letter from her hand. "I doubt he would have put them in a wooden staircase. If the house burned down, surely someone would find them. Augustus writes that he feels 'concretely sure' that the coins were where no one would find them."

Adrenaline surged through Meranda as she reached for the letter. "Concrete!" She looked at the judge and Glenys, who by their furrowed brows seemed completely perplexed. "Are there steps in the house made of concrete? The cellar perhaps."

Glenys and her father looked at each other, then raced to the back of the house. Paul and Meranda followed on their heels as they headed into the kitchen. They stopped at the door with the shelf above it.

Meranda took note of the tin box that she knew was void of the second pendant. "You said your pendant had been found behind the wall above the door?"

Glenys and her father both nodded.

"Another clue! Your pendant pointed the way to the cellar."

Glenys threw open the door to the cellar. "There are ten steps down. And each one solid concrete."

Meranda looked at the hammer and chisel in her hands. "I'm going to need something bigger."

Soon she was pulling a sledgehammer over her shoulder

and demolishing the first step. The concrete crumbled away easily, not the same quality as what modern-day builders used. At the bottom of the slab, a piece of leather began to emerge. Paul joined her, and together they clawed and chiseled at it until it was free. Meranda pulled the pouch out, opened it with shaky hands, and gasped at the two perfect gold coins with two pillars on one side and a crest on the other.

"Hello, welcome back to the family." She pressed them to her heart.

"Aren't there seven coins?" Glenys asked.

Meranda replaced the coins in the bag and tossed them to her, then leaned on the sledgehammer. "We found two of them. Augustus probably split them up in case someone found one batch. Anyone not knowing to look for seven would probably consider themselves lucky and not look anymore. So there could be one here"—she tapped the next step—"and two here"—she tapped another.

"Your Augustus was a smart cookie." Glenys sat on the kitchen floor and hugged her knees. "So let's see what's in the next step."

Meranda continued to pound the steps until she felt sweat trickling off her face. Paul offered to take over, but she held him off. "I need to do this."

He nodded, and she continued, finding two coins each in the next two steps and one coin in the eighth step. In the pouch holding the last coin, a note had been included. She carefully unfolded the ancient page, her heart pounding against her rib cage.

She read it aloud: " ' "Blessed be the God and Father of our Lord Jesus Christ, which according to his abundant mercy hath begotten us again unto a lively hope by the resurrection of Jesus Christ from the dead, to an inheritance incorruptible, and undefiled, and that fadeth not away, reserved in heaven for you, who are kept by the power of God through faith unto salvation ready to be revealed in the last time." First Peter 1:3–5. To all who find these coins, accept instead the perfect inheritance from our Lord and Savior Jesus Christ, who assures salvation and an eternal home where the treasure in your heart suffers not from moth nor rust, and where thieves do not break through nor steal. If the finder does not need these coins to survive, please hide them again for the next generation, and give them the opportunity to accept God's perfect incorruptible inheritance, Jesus Christ.'"

Meranda lowered the note, and while standing in the rubble of the stairs, leaned into Paul for support. He enfolded her in his arms and kissed her head with dusty lips. She was too stunned to think. This was bigger than she had ever imagined. Had she not accepted Christ in the hospital, she would have surely done so after reading her great-great-grandfather's words.

Glenys looked up at her father from her sitting position on the kitchen floor. He had been standing at the top of the stairs throughout the demolition. She spoke reverently, with a quiet tone one might use in church. "I wonder. We thought the inscription on our pendant was IR1.345, but what if the R was actually a P? IP.1.345—the verses in First Peter."

Judge Bernard sank to the floor. "Could be. The R always looked funny to me." He nodded and turned a dazed look toward his daughter. "I never put much stock in religious things. Your mother was in charge of that." He wiped his nose with a handkerchief and glanced toward Meranda. "This *game* has been going on for how long?"

Meranda carefully ascended the staircase, stepping only on those steps she hadn't destroyed. "Four centuries." She lowered herself to the kitchen floor, cuddling the coins to her chest, proud of her family for making the treasure hunt so much more than material blessing.

"Wow." The judge ran his fingers through his already disheveled hair. "I think I'd better look more into this God thing." He smiled at his daughter. "You think He'd take an old ambulance chaser like me?"

"Oh, Daddy." She threw herself into his arms and wept. "I wish Mom could know her prayers are being answered."

Paul looked up at them from the cellar floor. "She will know when all of you are reunited in heaven."

Glenys buried her face in her father's chest, where she managed a muffled, "Thank you, Paul."

"Um. . .wait a minute." Paul had out his notebook. "There's one more step."

"But we found all the coins." Meranda counted them in her hand again.

He picked up the sledgehammer and held it up to her. She leaned against the kitchen wall. "Would you? I feel as if my arms are coming out of their sockets."

His broad smile assured her that he was more than ready to play demolition. He spit on his hands, gripped the wooden handle, and swung at the step with all his might. The cement cracked. One more good whack. Then another. Finally he stopped to brush aside the chalky chips. "It's another pouch." He worked it from the cement and peeked inside, then drew out another note. A small grin spread across his face as he read silently.

Meranda's patience stretched as tight as the skin on a sun-baked mackerel. She stood with the other two at the top of the stairs, sure they must have felt the same. "Well? Is it another coin?"

"Nope. Read this note." He handed it up to her but kept the bag from her reach.

She read out loud, "'The Lord has been very good to me. I pass my bounty on and pray that the finder will use it as needed. Augustus Drake, Crossroads Bay, 27th day of March, 1907.'"

"That's my birthday!" Meranda felt her neck tingle. Was God redeeming the day for her so she'd have something good to remember?

Paul climbed up the steps and stood with her. "Open your hands."

She held out her palms, and he poured a cup full of yellow nuggets into them. All four said in unison, "Gold."

❧

Two weeks later Paul joined a church group of about twenty people who had booked the *Golden Hind* for a deep-sea fishing charter. Meranda had called him the day before to see if he'd like to learn how to fish. Deep-sea fishing had never been something he considered doing, especially in view of his aversion to boats. But he found himself excited about the adventure.

He also felt it a good way to market himself. He boarded with enough food to keep everyone happy and had his business cards in his pocket ready to hand out. An idea began to hatch as he worked in the galley. If Meranda charged for the food, he could provide snacks and meals on a regular basis. Currently, she only provided fresh bottled water and informed her guests they'd have to bring their own food but could use the galley.

With everyone on board, Meranda tucked a disobedient curl under her scarf, gripped the throttle, and pulled away from the dock. Paul had joined her at the helm and stood behind the captain's chair. He praised God that he'd conquered his fear.

Glancing to the deck below, he saw that the passengers all seemed occupied looking out at sea. This gave him confidence to flirt a little. The warm sun kissed Meranda's cheeks, making them glow, and he did the same. "Okay, your kitchen is good to go. I brought plenty of tapas for your guests to enjoy."

Meranda smiled. "I saw you cart the appetizers in. We can't possibly eat all that food."

"No, but whatever is leftover can be yours to snack on. You

know, something nutritious the next time you're out."

"Chips and cookies aren't in the major food groups? Not even the tiniest part of the food pyramid?"

"No. Those are convenient heart stoppers at best."

"I don't mind. Your food has changed my palate." She maneuvered the larger craft away from the dock and throttled up to head out to sea. "I loved Pop, but whenever we'd sail we would stop at the corner store and stock up on anything in a bag or a box."

Paul shuddered. "Plastic food. Yech."

Arrgh. . . Arrgh. . . . The pirate ring tone came from Meranda's hip pocket. She drew it out and looked at the caller ID. "It's Glenys."

"I wonder if she started her movie project."

"I'll put it on speaker so we can both hear her." She did so and yelled at the phone. "Hi, Glenys. You're going to have to speak up and quickly. We're just heading out to sea, so we may lose you. Paul is listening in."

"Hi, guys!" Glenys's smiling voice sounded from the speaker.

Paul waved at the phone, then realized she couldn't see him. "Hi, Glenys. What's up?"

"The authorities found the other pendant in Jessie's house. The night of my sister's wedding, she must have slipped inside when the police arrived for you two."

"Ouch, don't remind me. We had talked about the pendants being valuable together. And the pendants with the coins would have made a handsome booty. Oh!" Meranda's sudden excitement made her bounce in her chair. "That makes the treasure complete then."

"What have you planned to do with the coins?"

"Right now I have them in a safety deposit box."

"Are you going to hide them for the next generation?"

She glanced back at the lighthouse. "No, I can't risk anybody else losing his life. I'm going to donate them to the museum.

I'll include the research we found in the journals and the letters from Augustus."

"What about the pendants? They need to be on display, too."

Meranda fingered the pendant from the chain on her neck. Paul wondered if she would be able to part with it for the sake of history. She surprised him by agreeing enthusiastically.

"Maybe," she continued to talk to Glenys, "the curator will create a prominent display including the note we found with the coins. Do you know how many people will see that and be pointed to Jesus?" She rubbed her neck, and Paul knew she felt that tingle she always got when she solved a clue. He kissed her hair, proud of the shift she'd made from needing the coins at all costs to sharing the coins for Christ.

"I know you'll be blessed for that decision, Meranda." Glenys sighed. Was she remembering the tender moment with her father after the note was found with the coins?

Paul stood behind Meranda and massaged her shoulders, then kissed her hair.

"I'm blessed already, Glenys." She turned her head for a brief kiss. "Oh, and I have something to tell you."

"Go on, but hurry, you're breaking up."

"The camera I found in the wreckage proved to have evidence. Pop must have set it up in spy mode. It took several pictures in succession. Kingston never even realized it. It shows them pulling the boards from the cabin floor and Kingston finding a leather satchel under the boards. Kingston opened it. In the video, you could tell my dad was angry with him for doing so. You're not supposed to open items you find. They need to be processed slowly to keep the contents from deteriorating. He probably thought it was The Inheritance. Gold coins don't succumb to salt water. Thankfully, what was inside also doesn't corrode easily."

"Quickly! Tell me before I lose you. What was in the satchel?"

"Gold bars, ingots circa 1900. Augustus was probably going to use them to pay the crew. The video shows Kingston and my dad fighting over the bag. Kingston won. He must have then hidden it somewhere in the wreckage after he left Pop to. . ." Her throat caught just a little. "After he shut the door on Pop."

There was silence on the phone.

"Glenys?"

Nothing.

Meranda chuckled and put the phone back in her pocket. "If we went out of range before answering her, she's probably having a fit wondering what I said."

"I'm sure we'll hear from her later."

"Oh, no doubt."

Paul sat in the passenger seat. "I have a question. What about the third man on the shipwreck expedition with your father and Kingston? Was he in on it?"

"I didn't tell you? So much more going on, I suppose. The police questioned him. He seems to be in the clear."

"I've been thinking about Jessie, too. I think she targeted you. It was her idea to bid on the anniversary party that chartered your boat, you know, the first time we met."

Meranda offered a wicked grin. "How could I forget? There was the man of my dreams, upchucking over the side of my boat."

Paul almost wished he still had the seasick bands since she mentioned it. "Anyway, she was pretty forceful. Went behind my back to my grandmother after I said no. The two of them ganged up on me. Somehow she knew about the coins early on."

"Probably from her father." Meranda's gaze dropped to the gauges on the console. Paul assumed they would arrive soon at the waters she wanted to fish in. "I'm sure he bragged about trying to save my dad. It's possible that Jessie learned about my chartering business and since she was already a caterer, thought that would be a good way to snoop on my boat."

"Could be. She turned out to be pretty resourceful."

Meranda slapped the wheel. "I didn't get to tell Glenys that the police found the satchel at Kingston's house and that the *Crossroads Examiner* reported that he was sitting on the bars looking for a buyer."

"I wonder what Jessie's reaction to that was." He scratched the side of his nose. "She must not have known about the bars, otherwise why would she bother looking for the coins?"

Meranda frowned. "I think she would have been greedy and wanted it all."

Paul hated to admit it, but she was probably right. It hurt to think that such a talented chef could stoop so low. "Do you think she knew your father died at her father's hands?" He asked the question with reverence and added a stroke to her arm to let her know he understood her grief.

She shrugged. "You know her better than me."

He chose to think there was some good in Jessie. But after deliberating with himself, he came to the conclusion that given her split personality, it was possible she knew. The Jessie that held a gun on him that day was a stranger. He had other questions about her. "I'm wondering why she needed you if she knew where the shipwreck was."

"She may have known the location, but why risk going down there if I could lead her to a different place? Remember how gung ho she was at wanting to demolish the lighthouse wall?"

Paul laughed. "And I thought that was cute. So what do you intend to do with the gold bars in the satchel?"

"It isn't mine, is it? Kingston found it. With him going to prison, it will probably be locked up in red tape."

"It doesn't matter that he found it. That was Augustus's property, and you are his heir. I did some research after we found The Inheritance and the gold nuggets. According to treasure trove law in Oregon, the money is only granted to the finder if the suitable heir can't be found. But here you are!"

Meranda smiled. "Here I am."

He stood behind her again and kneaded her shoulders with his palms. He could almost feel where the weight of the world had once pressed on her there. She'd worn her pirate scarf, no doubt to keep her hair from blowing in her face, but her ponytail cascaded between her shoulder blades, dancing to the rhythm of the wind. Her bare neck entreated him to draw near, and for the first time he noticed a small tattoo. A butterfly resting upon a dagger. The two sides of Meranda Drake. He leaned in and kissed it.

"You know, you shouldn't distract the captain."

"I'm trying to shiver your timbers. Is it working?"

"Oh yeah." She tilted her head to the side to give him more neck to shiver.

He checked below to see if they were being watched, but everyone was intent on listening to Ethan as he handed out fishing rods. They must be close to their destination. Paul pecked her neck again. "Isn't there such a thing as autopilot?"

Meranda throttled the engine to a stop. "How's this?" She stood and hugged him close. Then she kissed him thoroughly.

When they parted, a whale spout just a few yards from the boat created a distraction for the other passengers. Meranda pointed it out. "Look at that."

Paul turned in time to see the whale surface, then slap the water with its tail fluke. "God's creation. Who could see that and not believe?"

"Not me. Not anymore."

They stood together watching a pod swim by and said a prayer of praise together, for all God had done in their lives and for all He was about to do.

eighteen

"This was a wonderful idea." Meranda snuggled with Paul on the deck of the *Romanda Jule* as they watched the water for whale pods migrating north. His arms warmed her while the autumn sun did not. A thin haze and a slight breeze enveloped them during their last excursion before Meranda would dry-dock the cruiser for the winter. "I've been so busy with charters lately, I've barely had time for you."

He kissed her ear. "I know. That's why I chartered my own tour."

"This isn't a charter boat, silly. I'm not going to charge you."

"Why not? I'm willing to pay."

"Then consider the food you brought aboard a catering job. How much do I owe you?"

He straightened and motioned toward the steps leading to the galley. "Those measly croissant sandwiches?"

"Yes, those and all the other times you've fed me."

"Fine." He settled back and pulled her close again. "We're even then."

She let the comment drift away on the seafoam and hugged his arm closer to her rib cage.

"I found a buyer for Augustus's gold ingots."

"That's great." His breath in her hair had an intoxicating effect. She could barely think straight, but she wasn't about to move.

"My sisters and I have agreed to open a foundation to help sailors and their families who struggle due to an accident at sea."

Paul squeezed her tight. "That is a very noble thing to do. I'm guessing you're naming it after your father."

She nodded and looked toward the lighthouse. "The Gilbert Drake Sailor's Fund. All those boaters who made fun of him because of his dream will whisper his name with respect."

"That honors Augustus, too. Sounds like something he would do."

Meranda let that sink in. She hadn't thought in terms of what Augustus would do, but what the Lord wanted her to do.

They drifted for a few more minutes, the boat gently rocking on the waves. Meranda thought about how, a mere five months ago, she was determined to find the coins at all costs. But after giving God the search, her priority changed. Even now, after finding The Inheritance, the coins weren't really what she was looking for at all.

"Thank you, Paul."

"For what?"

"For teaching me which path to take at the crossroads. Had I continued on the one where I was assured full control, I probably would have destroyed myself."

They sat in silence for a moment longer. Then Meranda continued. "I just realized it wasn't the coins I needed. They didn't validate my dad, nor give me peace. Truthfully, the one and only thing that makes me happy right now is that I've made peace with God. I was so angry with Him for taking my dad."

"And you're not angry now?"

"No, Pop made his own choices, chose his own crossroad. Just as I did when I decided to dive the wreck. God didn't kill him. If anything, God probably spoke to his conscience as He did mine and Pop ignored it—just like I did."

"However, you changed course, and that took more courage than your captain's heart ever imagined."

He scooted away from her, and she felt the whoosh of cool air where his body warmth had been. He stood and faced her, reached into his pocket, and took out a small box. As he lowered himself to one knee, Meranda felt the minnows inside her stomach beside themselves with loopy happiness.

"I'm not much of a sailor, and I learned a few months ago when you tried to teach me to fish that I really didn't enjoy it. . . ."

She giggled. He'd have to get over his fear of big fish before they tried that again.

"But what I do have is my love and respect for you. Captain Meranda Drake, will you marry me?"

She tapped her lip. "I don't know."

His smile fell, but he continued to hold the box out to her.

"Promise you'll make me paella whenever I want it?"

The grin returned. "Promise."

She pretended to think a moment longer, although she'd made up her mind before his knee ever hit the deck. Finally she let him off the hook. She threw her arms wide. "Yes, of course, yes." They embraced and kissed, neither willing to let the other go.

But Paul managed to slip the ring onto her finger with one hand while his other arm tucked her into his embrace. "I know it's not as impressive as your other jewelry."

"The pendant? It's not as heavy, either." She gazed at the diamond set in the simple gold band. She'd never been one for girlie jewelry, but this ring represented Paul's love for her, and that made her feel very feminine.

After several blissful minutes, Paul looked at his watch. "I hate to end this moment, but I have to work tonight."

"Blast! You'll have to take the helm because I want to keep looking at my ring."

He settled into the captain's chair with her by his side. As they neared Crossroads Bay, he headed toward the lighthouse instead of the pier.

"Where are we going?"

"I just need to make a stop first."

He pulled up to the new dock connected to the lighthouse property. The judge had it built just for Meranda so she could visit anytime. Paul hopped out and offered his hand to Meranda. *Hm.* Something was up. But she allowed him to pull her up the steep wooden steps. When they passed between the pillars, he stopped.

He took both of her hands and gazed into her eyes. "This is where my crossroad led me. The pillars were what convinced me to help you look for the coins. That decision, I believe, led us to today." He took her left hand, turned her toward the lighthouse, and shouted, "She said yes!"

People flooded out of the lighthouse. Meranda's hand flew to her mouth. She recognized her family, his family, their friends, and among them Glenys and the judge. At the house, Paul's catering crew began setting out carts of food.

She started to speak but found herself breathless. She barely noticed he was pulling her toward the house. Finally she found words. "I thought you said you had to work."

"I do. I'm catering an engagement party. Ours."

"How did you know I'd say yes?"

He kissed her once more, then said, "Faith."

Dear Reader,

When I was doing my research in Oregon, I was told that Oregonians are very protective of their lighthouses—that I needed to get every detail correct. That had me shaking in my tall black boots because I knew I would have to use creative license.

So it is with much trembling that I must tell you this. I decided to create my own lighthouse as a tribute to those along the southern coast. The lighthouse in my story is loosely based on Cape Blanco near Port Orford, and my location is a mixture of Coos Bay and Bandon. The lighthouse in Coos Bay, Cape Arago, is not open to the public.

I asked myself, how can I research a lighthouse that I can't get into? Hm. That was Meranda's problem.

She also couldn't get into the lighthouse, but unlike me, she didn't have the advantage of writing herself out of the situation.

Meranda's problems intensified when she found herself at a crossroad while searching for the coins. She could follow her way, which led down a dangerous path, or God's way, which meant she had to wait on Him.

Have you ever had a crossroad moment, that one important life-altering decision to either go your own way or God's way? How long did you struggle—or are you still struggling?— before you realized that God's way was the best, or as the verse states, the good way. . .where you will find rest for your soul?

My prayer for you is when you find yourself standing at that crossroad, that even though your way is more familiar, you will trust God enough to turn from the path of destruction and let Him guide you.

And who knows? Perhaps that path will lead you to your treasure.

Blessings,
Kathleen Kovach

A Letter To Our Readers

Dear Reader:

In order that we might better contribute to your reading enjoyment, we would appreciate your taking a few minutes to respond to the following questions. We welcome your comments and read each form and letter we receive. When completed, please return to the following:

Fiction Editor
Heartsong Presents
PO Box 719
Uhrichsville, Ohio 44683

1. Did you enjoy reading *Crossroads Bay* by Kathleen E. Kovach?
   ❑ Very much! I would like to see more books by this author!
   ❑ Moderately. I would have enjoyed it more if

   _____
   _____
   _____

2. Are you a member of **Heartsong Presents**? ❑ Yes ❑ No
   If no, where did you purchase this book? _____
   _____

3. How would you rate, on a scale from 1 (poor) to 5 (superior), the cover design? _____

4. On a scale from 1 (poor) to 10 (superior), please rate the following elements.

   ____ Heroine   ____ Plot
   ____ Hero   ____ Inspirational theme
   ____ Setting   ____ Secondary characters

5. These characters were special because? _____

_____

_____

6. How has this book inspired your life? _____

_____

_____

7. What settings would you like to see covered in future
   Heartsong Presents books? _____

_____

_____

8. What are some inspirational themes you would like to see
   treated in future books? _____

_____

_____

9. Would you be interested in reading other **Heartsong
   Presents** titles? ❏ Yes ❏ No

10. Please check your age range:
    ❏ Under 18   ❏ 18-24
    ❏ 25-34   ❏ 35-45
    ❏ 46-55   ❏ Over 55

Name _____

Occupation _____

Address _____

City, State, Zip_____

E-mail _____

BLACK HILLS BLESSING

3 stories in 1

The lives of three
modern women are
challenged by love
in the Black Hills of
South Dakota.

Historical, paperback, 368 pages, 5¾₆" x 8"

Please send me ____ copies of *Black Hills Blessing*. I am enclosing $7.99 for each.
(Please add $4.00 to cover postage and handling per order. OH add 7% tax.
If outside the U.S. please call 740-922-7280 for shipping charges.)

Name _____

Address _____

City, State, Zip_____

To place a credit card order, call 1-740-922-7280.
Send to: Heartsong Presents Readers' Service, PO Box 721, Uhrichsville, OH 44683

♡

HEARTSONG

PRESENTS

If you love Christian romance…

$10.⁹⁹

You'll love Heartsong Presents' inspiring and faith-filled romances by today's very best Christian authors…Wanda E. Brunstetter, Mary Connealy, Susan Page Davis, Cathy Marie Hake, and Joyce Livingston, to mention a few!

When you join Heartsong Presents, you'll enjoy four brand-new, mass-market, 176-page books—two contemporary and two historical—that will build you up in your faith when you discover God's role in every relationship you read about!

Imagine…four new romances every four weeks—with men and women like you who long to meet the one God has chosen as the love of their lives…all for the low price of $10.99 postpaid.

To join, simply visit www.heartsong presents.com or complete the coupon below and mail it to the address provided.

Mass Market 176 Pages

✂ -

YES! Sign me up for Heart♥ng!

NEW MEMBERSHIPS WILL BE SHIPPED IMMEDIATELY!
Send no money now. We'll bill you only $10.99 postpaid with your first shipment of four books. Or for faster action, call 1-740-922-7280.

NAME_____

ADDRESS_____

CITY_____ STATE _____ ZIP _____

MAIL TO: HEARTSONG PRESENTS, P.O. Box 721, Uhrichsville, Ohio 44683
or sign up at WWW.HEARTSONGPRESENTS.COM

to. As relieved as I am to have resolved differences with Lily, every part of me has been aching to find Melody. She's been the pursuer since I met her, and I'm excited to play the role this time around.

"I'd love to do that, Lily," I say, "But ,I gotta find Melody. You told me to kill myself, and that still is the second most disastrous conversation I had that night."

"That's a hell of an accomplishment. What did you say to her.?"

"You get the assist on this one, I used your word for her."

She finds this hilarious. "What a fucking idiot," she says, ignoring her role as creator completely. I swear my mother's influence on our social skills will live on forever.

"But here's the kicker, she makes me *feel*." The sobs from the next stall are starting to get distracting, but I've said enough hurtful shit to Harmony already. "Everything I thought I lost with Sara has come back. But Melody's so different that I don't feel like I'm replacing Sara, if that makes any sense. Melody just ... *gets* me."

"Then tell her that."

"I texted her, but she didn't reply. I'm just gonna head over to her apartment and—"

"Yeah, don't do that. It doesn't sound as romantic as you think."

"Ok, Cupid. What do you suggest I do?"

"Oh, I don't know. Maybe pick up the fucking phone and call her like a human being. Yeah, I think that sounds logical. Wouldn't you agree, little brother?"

"And what if she tells me to go to Hell?"

She sucks her teeth, my pessimism starting to wear thin on her. "Then I meet you at Rogue and we drown your sorrows in alcohol and chicken wings." I'm not against this, because the wings were better than they had any right to be.

"Wow. You have got to be the worst motivational speaker that I've ever come across. I'm just gonna go to her place, some things need to be done in person."

She laughs, "Either way, you won't have to deal with it alone. I promise. I love you."

We've never said I love you to each other. Ever. We have a love that's just understood, mostly through sarcasm and shoulder bumps. Any other time I would've laughed her off the phone, but tonight it just feels right. "I love you too."

After I hang up I sit on the toilet, staring at the ceiling, paralyzed by fear of calling Melody. It's the same fear I had in the airport bar a week ago. Even when you know the step needs to be taken, it doesn't make it any less scary. I view our week together as a success, even if she rejects me. Learning to feel again, after shutting all of your emotions down, is a bittersweet exercise. It hurts at the beginning, having to constantly remind yourself that human connection is a two-way street, requiring both effort and commitment. Like the first day at the gym, there's pain and the disappointment of not seeing immediate results. But once the initial tears are healed, and the pain reveals itself to be a necessary part of the process, it almost becomes an addiction. I'm tired of channeling my grief into self-destruction, it's more fun turning it to growth.

"I'm sorry for the things I said to you, Harmony," I say through the wall of the stall. We're the only ones in the bathroom, giving me the courage to speak freely. "I dehumanized you, and there's no excuse for that. You have value as a person, and Amy spoke highly of you." She doesn't respond, and I can't blame her.

The fear comes rushing back as my finger hovers above Melody's contact. I walk to the sink and rinse my face, but alas, the water doesn't rinse away the fear. My Uber's estimated arrival time is six minutes, so I fix myself in the mirror —trying to at least create the illusion that I have my shit together—before heading for the door.

"Miles, wait," a voice calls out from the stall.

The door to the stall unlocks, and Harmony steps out of the stall, still in her stage gear but carrying a small handbag like my mother's. I really need to stop subconsciously comparing dancers to the dominant females in my life. She's at the far end of the restroom, but close enough that I could tell she's breathing heavily. I dial Melody's number and wait for the dial tone. I step toward Harmony as 'Pictures of You' by The Cure starts blaring from her purse. Either somebody else in the world has impeccable timing, or I'm finally realizing something that's been standing right in front of me the whole time. I reach her just as the phone stops ringing, and I can hear her breaths, slow and fast, partially muffled by the mask.

I reach behind her and untie the mask, and my heart jumps like it did the first time I saw her. Melody looks apprehensive, unsure of my thoughts, and maybe a little scared that I'm gonna walk away.

But I try not to make the same mistakes twice, and I pull her into a long embrace.

There's a lot to work through, and stories to swap as we put together the pieces of the puzzle; each of us missing pieces that are held by the other. But, I just wanna live in this moment. She whispers over and over how sorry she is, and each time, I tell her she has nothing to be sorry about. It's not the most ideal place to reconcile, but nothing about us is ideal, and that's what makes it work. My phone buzzes, a message that my Uber driver is waiting for me. We both look at the notification, and I can tell she's scared that I'm gonna leave.

"You think you—"

"Meet me out back in two minutes," she says, before grabbing her mask and leaving the bathroom.

I leave right behind her and find the Toyota Highlander waiting for me by the valet. He agrees to switch the destination to my hotel and pulls around the back. Melody bursts out the backdoor, her stage attire replaced with a black tracksuit, and if I didn't tell the driver the plan, he would've assumed we robbed the place. Melody jumps in and we head off into uncertainty, but together nonetheless. None of that matters right now, because for once, I actually made a decision to do something because I *wanted* to, and it didn't bite me in the ass.

I guess this is it feels like to be on cloud nine.

TWENTY-ONE

ALL THE PIECES MATTER

BEING on cloud nine is a lot like drinking coffee.

The rush is initially satisfying, numbing you from the world and the responsibilities that come with it. But, if you ever watch a coffee commercial, upon closer review you realize it all takes place no later than noon. It's hard to convince people to buy your product when they know a crash is inevitably coming. Riding a wave of emotion is no different.

I don't know what the plan was when Melody came running out of the backdoor of Rogue. It didn't matter, because in that moment, in spite of everything, we'd found our way back to each other. But, as we sat in the back of the car in Manhattan traffic, the adrenaline levels out and reality buckles up in the front seat. We're holding hands and looking out of our respective windows, occasionally glancing at each other, unsure of where to start. But, since Lady Luck seems to be in my corner tonight, I start out with the only question I had.

"How did you know?" I ask. Her eyes meet mine, both of us understanding the question, and I feel her grip soften on my hand. "Not that it'll change my opinion of you," I reassure her. "But I feel like it's a good place to start."

She smiles, relishing the opportunity to spill the beans. "About a year ago, Lily started coming in to the club," she begins. *I knew it.* "She became a regular, and slept with about half of my coworkers. But, she could never convince me to come home with her."

"Because you don't like women?"

"I've played around before," she says with a smirk, which makes my mind race with possibilities. "But she wasn't my type, and I vowed to be done with toxic relationships. Once she knew it wasn't happening, we developed a mutual respect for one another. She stopped being pushy, unlike most of my customers, and I think she started to view me in a different light from the other dancers. Anyway, she'd come in and vent, telling me about her life, and that's when I learned about you."

Mentally I'm putting the pieces together, feeling even worst about the accusations I lobbed at Lily knowing that she played it straight. "This was before they died?"

Melody nods. "Yeah. She'd get really drunk and talk about how much she missed you, and the bond you two had. Then a day later she'd be complaining about you. I got the vibe that your relationship was complicated, but eventually she would've made the call. But, whatever happened between you guys didn't stop her from keeping up with your life. I mean, she showed me your whole Facebook profile."

"I can't believe she opened up to you like that."

"You'd be surprised how comfortable people are talking to someone wearing a mask."

She's not lying. It was different than any strip club I'd ever been to, but it was perfect for New York City. Adding masks to the mixture of dancers and alcohol created something like an exotic confessional, a place anybody with a few dollars to spill their darkest secrets, and create new ones as well.

"Six months ago," she continued, "she came in on a slow night, and she was a different person. Usually people come to the club to have a good time, see a little skin. You know, live the fantasy."

The timeline she's laying out lines up with their deaths, and hearing Melody describe it feels like I'm reliving it all over again, but through the eyes of someone else—like one of those Guy Ritchie movies where it shows different points of view of the same event.

"But sometimes, there are customers that give off a certain ..." she struggles to find the word. "... vibe. Like, you can tell they wanna go to a dark place, and take dancers along for the ride. I try to avoid those types, but most of the girls have a price tag."

I think back to earlier, about the customer throwing money at her face, getting rid of his own demons by projecting them onto somebody else, not realizing that putting it on someone else doesn't numb them.

"That must've been the night she found out what happened," I say.

"It was. She took it bad, coming in high, which wasn't like her. Lily always talked about reconciling with you, but she thought your life was going so well, she didn't wanna complicate things by pulling you back into your past. She thought the world of your kids though, and always admired that you managed to get away from your mother and create the life you wanted. Lily was rooting for you, Miles, and so was I."

Our eyes meet, and she squeezes my hand. "But you didn't even know me."

"I'd never met you, but I felt a strange connection to you. You had every excuse to become a terrible human being, think about it. But you turned your childhood into something beautiful. It's inspiring."

Hearing her describe my life as 'something beautiful' is an example of the dangers of social media. My Facebook profile was a digital snapshot of my life, cropped and shaped to my liking, masking my insecurities as I soaked in compliments from friends on how great of a family man I was.

"You're such a great Dad," one person would write, usually under a picture of me at an event with the kids.

"Sara is lucky to have a man like you," one of her friends wrote on an anniversary post.

Each comment was a rung on a ladder of bullshit, one that I gladly climbed with each post, before tipping over with their deaths. And since I was at the top of the ladder, the pain of the fall was harder. Anybody that knew us—and not many people did— would have seen my life for what it was; a group project I contributed the least amount of work to, but still came out with the same grade as everyone else. It's one thing for acquaintances to leave random comments under your photos, it's another to know that your previously estranged sister and future budding love interest thought you had your shit together.

"Melody," I say. "I know what it looked like, but I wasn't that great of a father, and even worse as a spouse."

"Maybe so, but you recognize that you should've been better, and that counts for something."

I'm starting to wonder what I'd have to say for Melody to walk away. Not that I want her to, it's more wanting to know where the line is, so I could go nowhere near it. I've called her a distraction, and outed myself as an average parent and spouse. But she keeps building me up, seeing the best in me when I don't see it in myself. This is so foreign to me that if the car suddenly pulled over, and the driver revealed it all to be an elaborate prank, I'd thank them for casting me and exit stage left.

"So, you knew about the suicide attempt before we talked about it?" I ask.

"Yeah, I pretty much heard about it in real time. I'd been prodding her to visit you anyway, but when she found out about that, everything went off the rails. I didn't see her again until the night she showed up with you, I figured she jumped on a plane and you guys figured it out."

Hearing Melody tell me how my suicide attempt had an effect on Lily is oddly comforting. Yes, a big reason for trying to kill myself was living without my family, but with therapy I can admit that it wasn't the catalyst.

I was afraid of being alone.

My whole life I've convinced myself that I didn't need anybody, and that train of thought served me well for many years. But as people, we can only function on self-love and stubbornness for so long, life and its obstacles make the road too treacherous. The human spirit is meant to be part of a village, sharing in the joys and sorrows, never letting the next person be overwhelmed. But relationships take effort, and I treated them like fire extinguishers, leaving them unattended until I needed them. When that emergency finally came, I was unprepared, frustrated because I had nobody to turn to. My entire life revolved around my family—at least when I wasn't being an idiot—and when they were gone, friends revealed themselves as acquaintances, and I learned what it felt like to truly be alone.

"I'd think about you a lot," she says. "Whenever I was having a bad day, I'd think of you out there, alone, trying to figure it out and it made me stop feeling sorry for myself.

Then I'd realize how stupid it was, dreaming of someone I'd never met. I repeated that cycle for months, and it drove me crazy."

"That would explain your face the first time I saw you," I say, remembering the shocked look she had that day in the coffee shop.

"I tried to forget you," she admits. "And then one day, I look up while working the morning rush and you were there, and I swear my heart almost jumped out of my chest." I laughed and mutter *universe* and she cut me off. "Exactly," she agrees. There was no reason we ever should've ever crossed paths, so I took it as a sign and stepped into the universe. I'm sorry I never told you I was a dancer, I thought you'd run ... like they all do."

"You don't have to be sorry," I say. "You're the first thing that's gone right for me in a long time. I should've trusted you and told you about my family, even though you already knew. Wait...you said they all run?"

"Its a running joke at the job between the dancers," she says. "Everyone wants to lay with you, but nobody wants to stay with you. It's almost impossible to have a healthy relationship when you're a stripper. Men are possessive by nature, so the idea that someone else getting to touch what a guy feels is rightfully his is a non starter for most."

I'm not sure how to respond to this, so I stay silent, hoping the silence will allow the thought to pass.

"I don't enjoy being a stripper, and I don't turn tricks like some of the other girls. You just get so tired of being hurt, you do anything to make sure you don't have to ask anyone for anything."

I'd never heard anything that resonated with me more in my life.

"After I left your place, I had a huge fight with Lily and

my Mother. I thought I lost you ... and I needed somebody else to feel that pain." The night replays in my mind, seeing my mother walk out without even putting up a fight plays over and over. "I told my mom it made me sick to know I needed her. Then Lily told me I should finish the job next time."

She laid her head on my shoulder, her way of letting me know she was there, but wouldn't pry if it was to uncomfortable.

"I packed my clothes and left for the airport, didn't even check out of my room. It's so easy to run away and start over when you spend most of your life being alone."

"You don't have to explain yourself to me, I get it," she assures me. "Why'd you come back?"

I place her hand on my wrist, now bare without the constant reminder of how far I'd fallen after Sara died. "I called my therapist in the boarding line," I say, laughing because Dr. Felt had won again. "I called her because I knew she'd talk me into staying, which I wanted to do anyway, and she made me realize leaving would only make the pain worse."

"Sounds like a great therapist."

"She is, she really is."

The Freedom Tower looms over us, which means the hotel is getting closer. The driver lets us out at the front and I make it a point to tip extra in appreciation for him not chiming in during our conversation. Things starts getting heavy about halfway up the elevator ride to my room as I took in every scent of her, neither of us burdened by the skeletons of our respective pasts. As I unlock the door she stops me, a look of fear paralyzed her while scaring me.

Does my breath stink?

Am I moving too fast?

Should we have gotten dinner first?

"It's alright if you can't stay because you have work in the morning."

"It's not that, I'm actually working the open mic tomorrow, it's just..." She's nervous, like whatever she's gonna say could ruin the night. "...just for tonight, can you forget that I'm Harmony?" she asks. "Please?"

The door beeps and a clicking sound echoes through the deserted hallway. My foot holds the door open as I look her in the eyes, and I can see the fear. Fear that I would be like the rest, that she'd be discarded in the morning to rebuild the wall she'd taken down for me.

"Melody..." I say her name, "I have no fucking idea what you're talking about."

She smiles and jumps into my arms, picking up where we left off in the elevator. I flicked the lights on as I carried her through the doorway. The auto close mechanism of the door does its job.

I'll remember to leave a five star Yelp review because of it.

TWENTY-TWO

LUCID DREAMS

"Is HE AWAKE?" a voice whispers gently.

"Touch his nose," another voice says, from a further distance than the first.

A warm hand clamps my nose shut, and when I open my eyes, my daughter Grace squeaks and jumps back. I realize I'm not in New York, but in my bedroom back in Colorado.

"Daddy, Daddy, Daddy!" Harry, exclaims as he bursts through the door, revealing himself as the second voice. "Daddy, you're awake, you're awake."

He always sends his sister to wake me, figuring I wouldn't be as angry with her.

Some things never change.

Harry spins in circles yelling my name, his body trying to keep pace with his mind. He tires himself out before joining his sister in my lap, jockeying for position with Grace before I convince them there's enough room for both of them. I embrace them both tightly, unsure of how I got here, but determined to hold onto them as long as I can.

"Daddy, why are you crying?" Harry asks, running his

fingers through the streak of tears I didn't realize we're falling.

"I'm just so happy to see you guys," I say, running my fingers through his curls, still in disbelief that I'm holding them again in our home. They're both in the footsie pajamas, prepared for both a playdate at home and a Walmart run.

"Daddy," Grace says. "We...um... made breakfast for you, and want to eat as a family. Please Daddy, please."

"Of course princess."

It always made me chuckle when she talked like that. Her little mouth so excited to say what was in her heart that it would come out in spurts, and in my head, I'd insert commas and periods. But she wasn't lying about breakfast, the scent of maple sausage , a staple in our family, wafts into the room. There will be a side of cinnamon raisin toast and cheese eggs to go along with it. To pass the time, they take turns being flipped on the bed, each giving demand on how they want to be flipped.

"Put me on your shoulders, put me on your shoulders," Grace screams and I oblige, her little hands gripping my ears for stability.

"I'll save you Wonder Woman," Harry says, using a running start to hit a drop kick to my stomach. He helps her off my shoulders and I slump onto the bed, letting them pile on, burying me under anything they can find.

I lay still under the mess of pillows as they celebrate slaying the monster, taking turns peeking under to make sure I'm not moving.

My heart is full right now. In this moment I'm being the father I should have been all along, instead of the one they saw in spurts. It's too late to make it right, but I can make this moment last, and for that I'm thankful.

I burst out from under their pile, roaring like a lion and

sending them running for cover. Grace hides on the side of the bed, waiting for her brother to emerge from his usual spot in the closet. Their unity during these battles was always a fascinating look into their relationship. They'd be thick as thieves one moment, then at each others throats the next.

"Morning there sunshine," a voice says from the doorway.

I turn and find Sara there, as beautiful as she was on our wedding day, a cup of coffee in hand, smiling like she always did in these moments.—when she finally saw the father she knew I could be all along. If I had to guess, she'd been standing there awhile. Whenever I'd have playtime with the kids, she gave us space, allowing me to stay in the moment, and not get distracted talking about things married couples talk about. I joked that whenever her love for me would run empty, she'd use these moments to recharge herself.

"Breakfast will be ready soon kids," she says to them. "Paw Patrol is on in the living room, gives us a few ok?"

They put everything back in its place and head out, racing to see who could get to the couch first.

"Bye babies," I say, feeling like the breakfast they spoke of isn't gonna happen. "I love you."

Sara jumps in the bed, placing her leg over my torso, our hands finding each other like they always did. She breathes deep into my neck, the Tahitian vanilla from her shampoo teasing my senses. There's much to be said between us, but I don't know how much time I have, so I take her in one last time.

"I've missed you," she says, before kissing me, starting from my neck and working her way up.

"I'm sorry," I tell her, "I'm sorry I didn't figure it out until it was too late."

She kisses me softly, and I notice she has tears streaming down her face, mixing with mine to flow down my neck. My foot finds the waistband of the fleece pajama pants I got her our last Christmas together, the ones she swore she'd never get back into after she had our third child. I slide them down, the warmth of her skin reminding me of the first time we made love.

I was so nervous back then, just the awkward guy from her chemistry class with a weird sense of humor. It was my first time, but she guided me through it, like she would do once we were married.

Sara guides my hand on her body, shivering as I run my fingertips up her spine. She holds my hand to her face, pecking softly, her shallows breaths warming my palm. The breeze of the ceiling fan meets the tears, creating a cold that makes me shiver. Sara smiles, rubbing my head and kissing my hand, never breaking eye contact.

"Miles," a voice calls.

Sara looks up in a panic, trying to figure out where the voice came from. It wasn't the kids, and the look on her face tells me we're the only ones in the house.

"Miles," the voice calls again, this time louder.

Sara is staring up, still in a panic, before a smile eventually forms on her lips. It's a sad smile, one I would normally see after she'd realize she couldn't talk me out of something. A smile of acceptance, of understanding that fate was at hand. She grips my hand tighter, tears fully streaming as it dawns on me what's happening.

"Miles, come on. Please, Miles," the voice pleads even louder.

"It's ok, Miles," Sara says. "We're ok, I promise."

The room suddenly turns bright, and I can barely make out her silhouette, the touch of her skin slowly fading away.

"Don't go," I cry out. "Please don't leave me again, I'm sorry."

"It's alright Miles," she says, fading away.

"I can be better, just don't leave yet," I beg, struggling to convey every regretful thought I've had since they walked out the door. "I'm sorry Sara. Can you hear me? I'm sorry, please come back."

"We're alright." It's almost in a whisper.

"Come back."

The room becomes too bright to make anything out as Sara keeps repeating assurances, softer and softer until she fades away.

"Miles, please wake up," the voice says.

A room is coming back into focus, but it's not my bedroom. The shape of a woman is coming into view. My hotel room begins to take shape, the sharpness of the lighting gleaning off the chandelier, illuminating the woman. She's holding my wrists, trying frantically to get my attention. I'm pulled into an embrace as she rocks me back and forth, whispering words I can't understand into my ear. It's a touch I have never known before, both comforting and reassuring. The woman isn't Sara, and she isn't Melody.

The woman is my mother.

TWENTY-THREE

THE TRAILS WE TAKE

I JUMP BACK without a thought to my position and crash into the night stand. As nice as this room is, I'm beginning to think it's bad luck.

The two times I woke up expecting Melody to be there I was greeted by a stripper and now my mother.

My heart pounds rapidly as Sara's last words replay I my head. She wanted me to know they were alright.

"Christ, Miles, are you alright?" my mother asks, rushing to help me up off the floor. "What the hell are you jumping for?"

"I saw them. I was back in Colorado, and I saw them." I get up from the floor, covering myself with a blanket before moving through the hotel suite, looking for Melody. "It was like they never left."

"Saw who?" she asks.

"Your grandchildren, Mom," I shoot back, annoyed that she isn't keeping up. But the dream is second to me finding Melody. Two rooms down in my search and not a sign of her.

"Miles, what are you doing?" She asks, staying right on

my heels.

As my brain reboots I remember that technically I'm still angry with her. "How about we start with ... oh, I don't know ... maybe, how the hell did you get in here is a good starting point," I continue to wander from room to room, hoping Melody just stepped away to make a phone call, or is enjoy the view. Panic takes hold with every room I find empty.

"She's gone Miles," my mother says, her tone carrying an authority that ends my search. "She let me in, interesting girl that Melody."

"You talked to her?"

She nods, "We chatted for a bit, she was in tears when I got here, so I gave her an ear."

The one person I have sex with woke up and had a conversation with *my mother* before disappearing. The best writers in Hollywood couldn't make this shit up. I run my fingers through my hair, dropping the blanket in the process.

"I forgot you were uncircumcised," she says conversationally, looking at my genitals. "Sorry about that."

"Mom, can I get a second?" I ask. "Just add it to the list of everything else you did wrong when I was growing up."

She gives me some time to get dressed, and I can hear her from the bedroom defending her skills as a mother. I'm sitting on the floor trying to collect my thoughts. Last night somehow surpassed my expectations, and not in the way one would think. It felt like a first date, with both of us free from the burdens we carried. I told her everything, filling in the blanks while being genuinely surprised at how much Lily knew about my situation. We talked about her night job, and all the weird things the customers would say to her.

"Does the stripper thing bother you? You can be honest," she asked.

"No, I mean, I'm the guy carrying a tragic past. At the very least, we're even."

"But does it change the way you see me?"

"It doesn't, but this is all new to me," I told her. "The feelings I have for you, my own insecurities, it's a lot to process. But there's something here Melody, and whatever it is, I wanna stick around for it."

After making love we laid out in the main room overlooking Central Park, the darkness of the park pockmarked by flickers of lights throughout. It was the first time since they died that I didn't feel alone in the world, and it was a feeling I thought was lost forever when Sara died. We opened another bottle and made love again, but it was different. Free from any secrets, we explored every part of each other, never breaking eye contact. If I never woke up, I would've died a happy man.

My mother joins me after awhile and takes a seat next to me on the floor. Despite all that we've been through, I'm happy she's here. Even if she's not the ideal person, it's nice having someone to process this with.

"What did Melody say, Mom?"

"She talked about the time you guys spent together, and how you made her feel. That reminds me," she says, pulling a piece of paper out of her handbag. "She had to run, but she said to give you this."

It was a letter, written on the hotel stationary from the nightstand. The handwriting is scribbled but legible, written in haste before I could wake up. I open it without a thought, desperate for information:

Dear Miles,
I'll start with an apology. Please don't take me
leaving as a sign of me not caring about you. In fact, I

*actually care about you too much, and it's why I'm
doing this. I was starting to wonder if my idea of
following the Universe's signs was a cop out for not
wanting to be vulnerable. But, then you showed up
and helped me understand that I was just waiting for
the right person. I'm used to men only wanting sex
before using my job as an excuse to rid themselves of
me. But you showed me that I have worth beyond the
stage, and for that, I could never repay you. Spending
time with you this week has made me feel emotions
I've never felt before. To be seen as a human being,
with feelings that matter, allows me to believe in
people again. To believe in love again. You did that
Miles. No matter how many regrets you have in your
past, know that you're a good person (and a great
lover too :-)). But, in my excitement to validate my
view of the world and experience intimacy, I ignored
your recovery in the process. I cast you unknowingly
into a role you aren't ready for, and I'm sorry for that.
If we never see each other again, I'll always look back
on our time together as the moment my life started to
make sense. This isn't goodbye. At least I hope it's
not. This is me trusting that when the time is right,
the universe will lead us back to each other.*

Love, Melody

I fold the letter up and fall into my mother's lap. She takes the letter and reads it, smiling for whatever reason and chuckling after handing it back to me. I join in the laughter, because life has reached the point where that's all I can do.

"What made you come back?" I ask, trying to avoid talking about Melody.

"Because I felt you needed someone in your corner."

"Great timing," I reply, immediately wishing I could take it back.

She moves my head and goes to the window, staring out in silence. "Why do you hate me so much?" she finally asks.

I was expecting a snarky remark like usual, but the question and the weariness of her tone catches me off guard. It hurts to know she feels this way, because I've never hated her. But, all the jabs I've thrown at her over the years clearly had an effect.

"I don't hate you, mom..." I trail off, unsure if the time is right for this conversation—or if I'm in the emotional space to have it. But, the alternatives are talking about last night with Melody and my dream, so it wins by default.

"Then what is it?"

"I just—I just don't know how to love you."

She shakes her head. "Wow, you know the absolute worst things to say to a person."

"Well, I learned at the foot of the master."

She opens her mouth for a rebuttal, but her heart gets the better of her mind. "That's fair."

In our minds, we build these moments with relatives into epic confrontations. I always imagined confronting my mother over the phone, drunk of course, because that's the only way to get through a conversation like that. But, over the last couple of days I've come to see her in a different light, and I'm still not sure if I'm buying it. That's unfair to her because she's really making an effort, even if her delivery isn't perfect.

"Now, isn't the time for this conversation," I tell her.

"Actually it is," she replies with a tone of authority reserved for parents. "I think we both know we should've talked a long time ago, and if we don't have it now, we never will. So, I'm gonna give you the chance to say anything you've ever felt, and while I hope it's not disrespectful, I understand it's been building inside of you for years, and I'm prepared for it."

Did she really just give me a license to curse her out? If Sara and the kids were still alive, I might've taken her up on it. But I can feel her sincerity, and the opportunity to build the relationship we should've had all along—the one I swore I never wanted but knew I did, the one that she apparently wanted as well. I wish Dr. Felt was here right now, because I don't even know where to begin. It's like walking into a messy bedroom, and there's so much junk you don't know where the cleanup should start. But you have to start somewhere, so you grab the first piece of trash and go from there.

"Alright, but where is this coming from?"

"You tell me, from what Lily and Melody told me, you've been pouring your emotions out all over the city this week. And you know, I'm always up for trying a new drink, especially when it's the talk of the town," she says. "Stop trying to change the subject, we're having this conversation."

"Fine," I say. I've thought about this conversation for the last fifteen years, even had a game plan going in, but my mind goes blank. This is going to be a difficult conversation either way, so I start with the biggest gripe I have. "I never felt like you really loved me."

Not the best start, I know, but I can tell by the look on her face this wasn't unexpected. She nods at this, and joins me on the floor.

"Do you remember what life was like before Greg?" she asks. "How I worked all the time, and the nights we had to eat at the shelter?"

We never talked about those times, they were something like our own little Great Depression. Mom worked two jobs during that time, doing everything she could, but always coming up just short. Our grocery money was dependent on tips from her waitressing gig, and when they didn't come in, we made the ten block trek to the shelter—where in exchange for listening to a sermon and helping with the cleanup, we got to eat.

"I buried those."

"I don't blame you, but dig them back up, because it's important. What was the best day to visit the shelter? I know you remember that."

"Monday," I said. "The broth was always better on Monday."

Mom smiles at this. "It really was."

Monday was delivery day, so everything was fresh. Even Lori, the chef, had a pep in her step on Monday. You could taste her passion for culinary on Mondays. Her food was always great, but on Monday, she cooked like she was competing for a Michelin Star. Lori was my first real friend, even though it was just her taking pity on my situation. She made me feel like I mattered, giving me important jobs and constantly building my confidence through positive affirmation, telling me I would rise above everything so many times I actually believed her. Lori knew the sermons held no value for me, so she'd sneak me out the back to make store runs with her to pick up little odds and ends for the kitchen. My shoes had holes in them, a hazard for working in the kitchen. So she bought me a new pair to keep in her locker, and after every store run, she'd give me five dollars with the promise of more if I could save it until the next time I saw her. That was how I learned the value of a dollar.

"I remember you running around that kitchen," Mom says. "You wore that little chef hat, as cute as you could be. But I was thankful for those moments, because you were able to get away from our situation and just be a kid." She rubs my head, and I don't pull away, both of us navigating new waters cautiously, but finding a new normal in the process.

"You know, I don't remember thinking about it like that."

"Why would you? You were a child. I can tell you this now, but I envied your relationship with Lori."

"Really?" I'm intrigued by this. I wanna chime in, but I'm mesmerized by the woman in front of me, processing emotions without sarcasm. The years before she married Greg were bleak, but they were also when we were closest, because all we had was one another.

"Yeah. When you were at home with me, all we talked about was survival. What bills were past due, if we were gonna be evicted..."

She averts eye contact, staring into the distance as she talks, and I'm trying not to move, using one of Dr. Felt's tricks. In the moments when I was reaching a breaking point, Dr. Felt was deliberate in her movements, knowing that if I broke concentration, I'd default to going into survival mode to finish out the session, making her job twice as hard next time.

"I put a lot of stuff on you that I shouldn't have. My drinking didn't help either. But when you got around Lori, you became a different kid, and I was thankful that she helped you forget why we were there to begin with. Sometimes I felt like you wanted her to be your mom, like you gave up on me."

"I didn't mean to make you feel that way."

"I know you didn't, Miles." She moves closer to me. "But all I'd known was broken relationships, and though I wasn't the best Mother, I knew I couldn't tell you that. You were just a kid. When Greg came along with Lily, I tried to build the relationship with her that I wanted with you, because I thought that ship had sailed for us already."

You can love someone your whole life, and realize you never really knew them at all. She's been Helen, a woman I loved, but didn't like. I'm realizing we'd spent all this time revealing our true selves to everyone but each other. But I don't feel any pain, because for once, I'm figuring something out before it's too late. The regret fades away a little easier.

"Well, you were right and wrong," I say. Mom looks puzzled by this. "I did give up on you, but it was later than you expected. Much later."

"How much later?"

I couldn't help laughing, sitting here like two detectives piecing together together the timeline of a crime. "Sopho-more year."

"You're kidding right? High School?"

"Yeah. At some point, I stopped trying. Seeing how close you were with Lily made me start counting the days until I could head off for college."

"Some of that was done to spite you, but I wanted you to see I could be a mother."

"But I'd already seen it, mom. You kept us afloat when we had nothing. I might have been young, but I could under-stand you were doing what you could." The awkwardness is gone, replaced by a curiosity as I try to process everything. "Since we're being charitable with our memories, I'll tell you something I've never told anybody else."

"I like where this is going. What?"

"Sometimes, I'd wish we were poor again. Crazy as it sounds, I missed the time when it was us against the world."

This revelation affects her. She just nods her head awhile, staring out into nowhere, trying to process everything. "I pushed you away," she says, shifting the tone of the conversation. "I tried to change, Miles, but I got scared and pushed you away. Even convinced myself I was teaching you how to deal with life. Every time I got it in my head to have this conversation with you, I'd panic."

"You still could've tried."

"And what would you have said?" she asks. I don't have a response because she's right. I would've blown her off, or made up an excuse to get off the phone. She was my antagonist, even more than my deadbeat father. I could force her to watch my growth in real time, using her grandkids to keep her hostage in the audience. I spent so much time trying to flaunt this persona to her, that I neglected them because I needed her to believe I was something I wasn't. Cutting her off was too easy. But keeping her on the fringes of my life— close enough to peek, but far enough to feel excluded— gave me an intimate look at the effects, like she did to me in high school. But that's the tricky part of harboring resentment, it damages everyone but its intended target.

"I'm sorry too, Mom," I say. "I've said some hurtful things to you over the years—"

"Water under the bridge," she interjects. "Life's too fragile to chase things we can't change. Let's just move forward."

"Done."

She caresses my face, and I give her the moment. "Can I ask you something?"

"You can ask me anything."

"How was last n—"

"You can ask me *almost* anything," I say fore she can finish. Mom raises her hands to signal she's leaving it alone. *Oh, what the hell.* "It was awesome."

"Ok, so what's next?"

Fuck. I couldn't let good enough be, I had nineteen on the blackjack table and got greedy. I fall into her lap, wishing I could've woken up and caught Melody. She slipped out of my life just as gracefully as she entered it, leaving feelings behind that I'll never forget. I spent the week chasing Melody around the city, and it's easy to think it was all for nothing. But in the process—from the bar to the record shop, and up until the moment I slid the mask off her face—I found something I didn't know I was looking for.

I found myself.

But in the process of finding myself, I lost her. The guy that walked in that coffee shop, with the heavy heart and shoe full of dog shit was gone ... or should I say fixed? Either way, he's better because of her, but she'll never see the fruits of her labor because he figured it out too late. A cruel twist of irony that I'll never get over.

"It's over, Mom," I say. She glares at me like I'm an idiot before grabbing Melody's letter and clearing her throat. She begins to read it out loud line by line, pausing at passages she thinks are relevant, punctuating them with a quick glance that drives home her insistence that I'm an idiot. During certain sections, she smiles, and I imagine Dr. Felt would smile while reading it as well. I'll imagine her face with every milestone I reach for the rest of my life.

"'*This isn't goodbye. At least I hope it's not. This is me trusting that when the time is right, the universe will lead us back to each other. Love, Melody.*'" Mom folds the letter and puts it back in the envelope. "Now—" she places the letter firmly on my chest. "—exactly what part of that letter says that it's over? Because I can't find it."

"You wanna be my mother, or you wanna be my therapist?" I ask.

"I wanna be whatever you need me to be, Miles."

The sincerity in her voice makes me regret the years I spent believing she was the bane of my existence. But, I think she's a little too optimistic about this situation.

"It's not as simple as it sounds," I say. "She's telling me to work myself out, and *maybe* it'll work out."

"What's there to work out?" She gives the rundown on my life. "Lily's been taken care of, I was never part of the equation to begin with, but we worked that out. If you left the city right now, the only thing you'd regret is Melody."

"You're not getting it," I say, frustrated. "She doesn't see the world like everyone else. I appreciate what you're trying to do, but she said the universe would lead us back to each other. That doesn't happen overnight."

She distorts her face in disgust. "The universe could drop that fucking chandelier on top of us too." She moves from under me, stand over me and puts her foot on my chest. "Listen, I talked to that girl for an hour, and she cares about you in a way that most people spend their lives searching for."

"But she—"

She balls her fist up to silence me. "This is the part where you shut the fuck up, and let me be a mother." She seems determined to make up for lost time, even though we agreed to move forward. "Listen, the universe did bring you together, and I'm thankful for it because she's perfect for you."

I don't know what they talked about, but it clearly had an effect on my mother. In my lifetime I've brought home six girls to meet her, and until now, only Sara has gotten the stamp of approval.

"But bringing you together isn't enough to sustain it. You watched me struggle for years trying to find what you're walking away from." She bends and takes my head in her hands. "Love is too precious to be left to chance. Do you understand me?" she pleads, shaking my head.

She continues before I can agree.

"You can't trust that it's just gonna work out. Relationships are too complex. And yes, luck got you to the door, but it can't make you step inside." She recites the last line of Melody's letter one more time. "That isn't telling you to wait, Miles. She's telling you to trust your feelings. If you don't go find her, what do you expect her to do? What does that tell her?"

"That she doesn't matter," I say. Mom nods, and moves her foot so I can get up. There's a knock on the door from room service, and Mom leaves to deal with it.

I find my clothes and jump in the shower, using every minute of this solitary time to summon the courage to go talk to Melody. The hot water gets the blood pumping to my brain and panic starts to set in.

What if I'm wrong?

It's easy for my mom and everyone else to tell me how stupid I'm being. They weren't on our dates. They never looked into her eyes as she told the story of her upbringing, the events that led her to believe what she does. If she turns me away, it's me—not them—that's going to have to deal with the heartbreak. Sure, they'll be there to support me and say the right things, like my other friends after the car accident, but they won't have to deal with the fallout. The late nights when you do a mental play-by-play of every moment spent together, wondering what you missed that made it all go wrong. They don't have to avoid certain places because the memories are too painful, or skip songs on a playlist because it opens the wound again.

But at the same time, I know I have to see her again. I could ignore it, convince myself that it wouldn't have worked out any way, but I know myself. Loose ends are fertile ground for self destructive behavior, and knowing I walked away without even trying will haunt me, casting a shadow over any relationship in the future. If I don't have the heart to go after her, then I wasn't worthy of having her to begin with. The fear of rejection is strong, but with a solid playlist and a night out, I'd eventually get over it. But I've lived with regret—it's practically been my roommate for the past six months—and the feeling of knowing you didn't do everything you could is one that I don't wish upon anybody.

The water is getting cooler, a reminder that I've taken long enough, and I get dressed quickly. Mom asks me if I want a shot for my nerves and I consider it, but politely decline, wanting my mind as clear as possible.

Mom gives me a once over, licking her fingers and pinning down wayward eyebrow hairs.

"Alright," she says once she's satisfied, "let's go find your girl."

TWENTY-FOUR

COFFEE AND CONDOLENCES

"You're officially on the list, Little Brother," Lily says triumphantly, returning to the table from the bathroom. "You're in the show."

"Just like that?" I ask, impressed. "How'd you manage that?"

"Even got you the prime time spot at the end of the night. So, don't ever say I didn't do anything nice for you."

"That's not what I asked, Lily."

She realizes I'm serious and comes clean, "Alright, I know the guy that runs it. His name is Mark, and he kinda has a thing for me."

"And?"

"And ... I might've told him I'd suck his dick if he put you on the performance list tonight. So, no pressure."

"No pressure? You don't even like men," I remind her.

"Yeah, I could see how that might be a problem. Unfortunately, telling him that didn't seem conducive to what we're trying to accomplish." She grabs my cheeks. "So, maybe you should stop worrying about what I'm doing with my mouth, and focus a little bit more on what you're about to be doing with yours. Ok, Shakespeare?"

Before I can respond, our mother returns from the hostess stand. I think she's annoyed, judging by her pursed lips. "Can you believe they charged us gratuity ... on three people?"

"Really?" Lily replies. "That's what's pissing you off? Not the twenty-one dollar Bud Light?"

Mom shoots her a look of disgust. "I can handle New York City prices, but it's understood that gratuity is only on parties of eight or more," she complains.

"I guess you're right," Lily concedes. "Who are we if we don't stand by our morals?"

"You just conned someone out of an open mic slot by pretending that you'd give him a blow job," I remind her.

"I believe I did that to help my little brother find his muse," Lily says. "But, as always, you're more concerned with the methods instead of the results."

"Will you two give it a rest?" Mom practically begs. "We haven't been back together a whole day and you guys are already at each other's throats."

We leave the restaurant and walk through Central Park, passing the spot where Melody and I had our first date. It feels like a million years ago when I think of how our relationship has grown since then. I laugh looking at the bench I hid behind, unsure if I could go through with the date. Or the bike stand, where I thought she was nuts for asking me to ride through the city.

"You guys go on ahead," I say. "I'm gonna hang out here for awhile, get ready for tonight."

They exchange glances of uneasiness, probably thinking I'm gonna use it as an opportunity to skip out on the open mic, but I assure them I just need some time to prepare for tonight. We agree to meet at Romancing the Bean and they head off, leaving me on a bench in the company of the squirrels.

I spend some time jotting down notes of things to say tonight. I haven't written a poem since high school. I lack the coordination to make a beat poem, so I settle on something like a letter. The words come flowing out of me. Narrating the last few months of my life as a spectator helps me appreciate the journey. Panic creeps in and out, fear of humiliating myself, or Melody telling me that the timing isn't right.

I find solace in the fact that if it goes wrong, I can shave my head and move to Thailand, where the exchange rate will allow me to live comfortably for the rest of my life as a bartender named Paco.

* * *

Under normal circumstances, I would enjoy the open mic night at Romancing the Bean. The clientele is more diverse than the morning regulars, with the hurried young professionals being replaced by middle age dreamers looking for fun night out without the stress of going to a bar. Lily is outside smoking when I arrive, and I can tell she's already had a couple drinks.

"I bet Mom you wouldn't show up," she says. "It wouldn't be the first time I lost out on something I was sure about. How you feeling?"

"Not as nervous as I thought I would be," I tell her. "Where's Mom?"

"She had to use the restroom. Don't worry, I'm making sure to run interference if she goes near your girl. She looks sad by the way, your girl."

I'm not sure if this bodes well for my chances or not, but

I'm happy to know the four bowel movements I had due to butterflies weren't for nothing. "We should go inside," I say. My spot was in the next fifteen minutes, assuming it's running on time.

"Hey," she says, "before we go in, and I mean this in all sincerity, I'm proud of you. If she turns you down, know that you won't have to deal with it alone." I pull my phone out and hold it up. "What are you doing?"

"Say what you just said one more time, but do it real slow," I tell her. She frowns and gives me the bird. "What? If I told mom you said something that beautiful, she'd never believe me."

We go inside and find our mother with a table close to the door. I see Melody, but I'm at an angle where she can't see me. I could tell something was off, but she was still efficient in her work. Somehow, she's even more beautiful tonight than the morning I met her. Maybe it's because I know her story, the scars that made her who she is, or the tender moments when she lets her guard down—like the moment right before I carried her into my room. People are much more beautiful when they're flawed, I think.

The act on stage finishes to polite applause and is relieved by the MC, Mark. He tells some lame jokes and has an arrogant persona. I make a mental note to have Lily record the moment she tells him she's not holding up her end of the bargain. He introduces the next act, a middle aged guy, Jerry, who comes to the stage with his acoustic guitar. He kinda looks like an out of shape Tom Hanks, but he has surprising range in his voice. He play three Beatles songs, closing with 'Hey Jude,' extending his time by singing the chorus multiple times. Mark appears on stage again and takes the mic.

"Give it up one more time for Jerry." The crowd gives

him a respectable ovation and Mark moves on. "Alright, we're down to our last performer of the evening, and for the first time in awhile, we've got prose poetry." The crowd starts snapping their fingers in unison. "Give a nice welcome to Mr. Miles Alexander."

I made sure to keep my eyes on Melody during my introduction to gauge her reaction. Hearing my name, she immediately looks up, and we lock eyes as I walk toward the stage. She's shocked. But, I still can't tell if it's the good kind. The applause from the crowd brings back the butterflies, and internally I start to panic as I fiddle with the mic stand. I'm breathing heavily, with a heart rate that's doubled in the past forty-five seconds. I sound like a pervert as my breathing blares over the PA system. My eyes find Melody's again and I remember that moment by the water, the first time I realized I was falling for her. I take my phone from my pocket, close my eyes, take a deep breath, and exhale slowly. I get a few laughs but when I open my eyes, I can see Melody has moved closer to the stage.

"Sorry, I'm a little nervous about this, so bear with me."

"You got this," someone calls from the audience.

"This piece is called Coffee and Condolences." I tell them, taking a deep breath and diving in.

"I've loved Coffee for most of my life. The smell of of a fresh pot, the jolt it provides to otherwise average mornings. I felt all of that before I ever had my first cup, and when I did, I was hooked. You see, I've always been a runner—jumping from one thing to the next, never satisfied, never appreciating what was in front of me. And Coffee fueled those runs, keeping me alert, eyes forever trained on what's next. It was an

*unhealthy relationship where I was giving more than
I was receiving."*

I sneak quick glances at Lily, Mom, and Melody, each of
them glued to me. I continue:

*"It wasn't until the crash—when I was forced to slow
down—that I understood how toxic the relationship
had become. All the events I missed, people I had
taken for granted, because I didn't wanna slow down.
Ashamed and heartbroken, I went looking for something to replace it, and that's when I met Condolences. It was a whirlwind romance; the Condolences
came so swift, flattering me and giving me a place of
comfort to feel sorry for myself, until she revealed
how fickle she could be, almost killing me. So here I
am, a life spent running, now on the brink of death
because the one I replaced was worse than the other."*

I can see Lily and Mom crying, but I don't look at
Melody. I can't look at her, so once again, I continue:

*So I have two vices, each pulling at my soul from
opposite directions, each offering its own tragic
ending. I needed help, but all those years running left
me with nobody. So, I had to settle for something I
never saw coming. I had to settle for a distraction.
She was everything I ever needed, even though
Condolences had told me I'd never be happy. When
Coffee told me I was ready to run again, she laced up
her shoes too. I guess what I'm trying to say is, I'm
thankful for the Coffee and Condolences, because*

without them, I'd be too blind to see what's right in front of me."

The applause is surprising, but appreciated. My breathing returns to normal as I lock eyes with Melody.

We gaze at each other for seconds, but it feels like forever.

Finally, through my tears I can see it, the faintest hint of a smile.

So I take my cue, say a silent prayer for luck, and step into the Universe.

ACKNOWLEDGMENTS

Truth be told, my list of acknowledgments for this book could run as long as the book itself. First off I wanna thank my wife Paula. At times she's had to keep our three children occupied so I could chase this dream of being a writer. To Xander, Naomi, and Chase, everything I do is so that your smiles can shine brighter everyday.

For Ms. Andie Hartz, in 7th grade you fostered my love for reading and writing as my English teacher and all these years later I hope this book makes you proud.

To Dr. Iver Arnegard and Juan Morales, you guys were the best writing professors a guy could ask for. Thank you for teaching me how to channel the pains and emotions of life and turn it into something creative.

Matthew Hanover, I don't think there's enough words to express my gratitude to you. I was inspired by your work and you've taken the time to help me through the entire process, treating this project as if it were your own. Our conversations and debates about everything under the sun have been one of the highlights of this process. Ian Shane and Matthew Norman are two other authors that took the time to offer advice and encouragement. I promise to always pay it forward if another author comes along looking for an ear.

To my editor Sarah Jane Villanueva, I expected an editor and found a lifelong friend. Thank you for taking on the duel role of editor and therapist.

Jennifer Fleming, you were the first person to believe in this project, thank you for always encouraging me to keep writing.

Thank you to my team of authors and beta readers. Angelique Bosman, Sarah Neofield, Amy Noelle Smith, Maryann Tippett, Ava January, Kristen Granata, Nikki Lamers, Anngie Perez, Melizza Khan, Ric Lucero, Hannah Pearson, Segan Falconer, Jeremy Reed, Leighann Hart, Lauren Mae, Natalie Wright, Nikki Carter, Ethan Rodriguez, and Noelle Davenport.

And finally, if you bought this book and made it this far I have to thank you, my readers. I hope you enjoyed my book and will leave a review. Knowing you took the time to purchase during a pandemic no less) and read my work means the world to me. If you enjoy it, feel free to drop me a line on Instagram.

ABOUT THE AUTHOR

Wesley Parker has enjoyed reading his entire life. When not writing he can either be found making a mixtape, engaging his fandom of Philadelphia sports, or hanging with his wife and three children.

He can be reached on Instagram @weswritesforfun and on Twitter @arigold710.